From Zaftig to Aspie

From Zaftig to Aspie

DJ Kirkby

Published in 2008 by YouWriteOn.com

Printed & bound by YouWriteOn.com

I am certain that life must be written in pencil for it seems that nothing is ever so perfect that it can not be improved upon nor is anything ever so awful that it can not be rectified in at least some small measure.

Birth day

My mom birthed me during the wildest mid-summer thunderstorm she had ever experienced. I slipped out of her body just as the nurse, who had told mom she couldn't possibly be ready to push yet, went through the doors at the far end of the corridor. Born as life intended for me to go on, my life continued to be a series of unintentional dramas.

Growing up in Canada during the 60's and 70's, with a hippie mother, wasn't the stereotypical hippie lifestyle of 'peace and flowers in your hair' that you might expect. I had been born with a disability that did not get classified until the mid 1980's and I blundered through life trying to figure out why I behaved and felt different from most everyone I met, until I was diagnosed with Asperger's syndrome at the age of 40.

This book begins with my earliest childhood memory. While writing about my childhood I have tried to reconstruct it as accurately as possible. I am happy to admit that I have had to use literary license when reiterating conversations or sequences of events but I have tried to do so in a way that accurately reflects how I thought, felt or behaved when interacting with others and also to be as truthful and accurate as possible when it comes to other people's behaviour.

Welcome to the story of my blunders. Although I seem to have gone about a lot of my life from back to front or right to left, it seems to have worked well for me and I hope this book fills you with a sense of belonging and inspires you to endeavour to achieve your dreams. For those of you who do not already exist somewhere on the Autistic spectrum, I hope you enjoy your visit to the parallel world of Autism.

Burying bumblebees

The humidity was awful during the summer of the year I turned four. Moist and almost thick, it coated my skin like a layer of warm oil. I felt as if I was trying to draw breath through a wet towel; each hot intake a struggle. Because of the generalised discomfort, mom had sublet our apartment and told me we were going to a farm near the ocean. She had arranged to help out while we were there in trade for our lodgings and food.

It was hot and dusty on the sides of the roads through the Prairie Provinces. My mom and I were hitchhiking across Canada to spend the summer by the sea. People hitched a lot in those days. Why? I don't know, perhaps it was safer then, perhaps less people had cars, certainly fewer people worked and maybe for this reason could afford the time it took to drift around the country at a leisurely pace. We were not the only people with their thumbs out on that road in 1973 and the more social ones moved amongst the clusters of fellow hitchhikers chatting and sharing road tales.

My memory tells me the heat was exceptional on that stretch of highway. We had just passed through Regina, or 'vagina' as I insisted on calling it. The road shimmered in the heat and the ripe wheat stalks in the fields stood still as the sun removed every last drop of moisture from them, creating a Province wide fire hazard.

In the haze of the heat, we waited for a car to stop and I occupied myself by burying bumblebees. I don't know why there were so many dead on that dusty shoulder of the highway. Huge fat things they were, their bright yellow stripes alternating with brown. Being an enlightened mother (or perhaps just too hot to be bothered by my silent antics), she let me amuse myself in this manner without admonishment; occasionally encouraging me to drink water from our canteen.

My white curls bobbed and bounced as I bent and probed with the stick clutched in my fat fingers, meticulously scooping a bee sized resting place for each plump furry corpse in the dust under the pebbles. On top of each dusty bee grave, I placed a dandelion flower head.

The next car that picked us up had a 12 pack of chocolate Ding Dongs and my mom let me accept first one and then another, when offered by the driver. I interpreted this unheard of treat as a sign of gratefulness for my kindness, from whichever Gods were responsible for Bumblebees. Sinking back onto the hot cloth seat, I ate the melting chocolate, cream and soft cake as the dust billowed past on the road edges stirred by cars' passing wake. Then thumb plugged in my chocolate flavoured mouth, I succumbed to sleep as the burning air blasted in through the car windows.

Where the sea otters played

One day a week or so into our holiday, I grew bored watching my mom busy at the stove helping to preserve some of the farm's harvest. Her cheeks were glowing from the heat generated by the pressure cooker. Inside that hissing, steaming pot was the first batch of antipasto preserves from the brightly coloured vegetables grown in the farm's garden. I thought of this place as 15 acres of freedom and other than one 'no go' area, I was allowed to wander around at will. No one seemed to worry about children going off on their own in those days. I feel saddened by my children's' loss of which they will never be aware; that freedom we had as children born in the '60's which no child today, including my own, is granted.

The only restriction on my freedom was the 'no go' area of the forest. I expect that was partly because it would have been easy for me to get lost but I don't suppose for one minute that was the only reason why they were out of bounds. I had seen the marijuana crops growing in the clearings when I had gone walking with the adults. I had been told these were to be kept a secret and not to be talked about when strangers were around. They said they were special treats only for the adults on the farm and that they didn't want to share them. Okay I understood that, I didn't like to share my special treats either!

The rest of the land was splendid beyond words; with its' huge vegetable and berry garden, the orchard with fruit and nut trees and the sea views from the top of the hill where the grapes grew. The sea was just over a mile from the end of the drive. It was a pleasant walk down the hill, along gravel roads whose dust was firmly settled as cars rarely passed the house.

The forest began on the other side of the ditch that traced the road. Often I saw deer standing and looking innocently wide eyed round them, appearing in awe of their surroundings but perhaps they were just wondering why the forest had suddenly ended. The breeze which seemed to constantly rustle through the pine needles carried a subtle note of the salty and somewhat sweet scent of damp driftwood.

As I approached the sea that fine day, I got my first breathtaking view of the otters. There was an A- framed house, its' cedar shingles grey with age, which sat on crushed shell Mandan Indian land. It was on this land, safely near the water, that the sea otters played. I stood and watched them scampering about, chasing each other across the gentle incline, running up the steps onto the porch and seeming to vanish into the shadows, before emerging again. I walked over and then onto the land.

Distracted by the crunch those ancient shells made under my feet, I didn't notice the young male sea otter approaching me. Quick as a flash he darted over, spun round and raced away. I crouched down, hand outstretched to try and entice him over as I would do with a cat. He ran over, nipped me hard on the fingers and began to head off but paused when I shrieked! I started to cry when he came closer, and afraid he would hurt me again, I stamped my feet in an attempt to scare him away.

'Be calm child, I will not allow you to cause harm on this land where the sea otters play'. The voice, carried on the breeze, seemed to come from the shadows of the porch. Concentrating on that area, I could see her, sat on the bench wrapped in a huge grey blanket.

'Why did he bite me?' my voice trembled slightly.

She leaned forward as she laughed; the light catching her eyes, just noticeable within the folds of her face. Her cheeks were as creased as the dried apple dolls you could buy this time of the year.

'He was inviting you to play with him, much the same as you would by tugging on a friend's hand'.

She paused and we breathed a while, then...

'He will come back when you show him you mean no harm'.

I was instantly respectful of this woman, her wisdom apparent in the measured tones of her voice. Instinctively I longed to feel the comfort of her arms around me for I knew she would be warm and soft and that she would know how to hug away any worries. Instead I drew in a deep breath and crouched down with outstretched hand to the otter that was still nearby.

His response was so swift that I almost shrieked again. This time when he nipped me, I was expecting it and it didn't hurt as much as I'd remembered. My breath whooshed out, rather noisily with relief, which startled him into bolting a few steps before his curiosity made him return. His thick fur was dark brown with lighter guard hairs and his whiskers were white. He looked like a cuddly toy even though he was more than 3 feet long. We were young; curious, playful and inventive enough to be able to enjoy each other's company until it was near dark.

That evening I stood on the porch of the A-framed house, watching the otters enter the sea and begin to hunt the oyster beds for their evening meal. Then I walked back up to the farm with the wise woman who had phoned earlier to let them know I was with her and the otters. She stayed for supper which consisted of fragrant pumpkin stew served in the hollows of individual warm loaves of rye bread. This meal fascinated me, especially the top of the loaf which acted as a lid and I played with lifting and lowering it till it grew soggy from the steam. It was the first time my mom ever finished eating before I did! She teased me, cheering and singing a victory song. I ate then, savouring the stew before enjoying each bite of that juicy loaf of rye bread.

I waved goodbye to the living apple doll of a woman, leaning against the warm wood of the door and tiltling my hand side to side as she walked down the drive. She was making her way back to her home by the sea with the help the bright moonlight. In her hand I could see she carried a little burlap bag onto which shells and beads were secured and into which the adults had tucked some of the special treats which grew in the forest clearings.

At the time I thought nothing of the special treats inside her bag, though I did desperately want a pretty bag like that to tuck my own treasures into! I had learnt that night that she visited the farm often and I looked forward to seeing her again. Looking back now with the knowledge of the modern increase in prescribed cannabis for terminal cancer and other painful illness; I realise that she was a wise old woman indeed as it must have worked wonders for the relatively minor, normal aches and pains that old age had brought her!

Cinnamon tears

Late autumn and we were back in the city. The weather had cooled and mom's leave of absence from work had ended. Cinnamon was babysitting me. She was a runaway hippie teenager who had the good fortune to hook up with my mom's group. She always happy for me to play with her beautiful hair, the colour of which I later learned was called Auburn, although at the time I thought she was named for the colour of her hair.

In the early afternoon she sent me for nap though I suppose she probably needed one more than me. I had been on the go constantly, wanting to play forts, to read books to her and to talk, talk, talk. I bombarded her with an endless series of questions and lists of rules to invented games, which I expected her to enjoy with as much enthusiasm as me. From the diminishing enthusiasm with which she answered my queries, I was aware that her patience was beginning to wane. I loved my naps anyway so I went off without a fuss to snuggle down under my blankets, sucking my thumb contentedly and cradling my Chewie doll.

The apartment was silent when I woke and I set off on a wander to find Cinnamon. I too was quiet as I was still sleepy and so I padded silently around searching for her rather than calling her name. I looked in the living room, saw no one, gave the cat a pat and then went into the kitchen. The kitchen and bathroom were empty as well as my aunt's room as she and my cousin were away for the weekend. I made my way to the room at the front of the apartment. It sat to the left of the front door, it's floor to ceiling window giving a false appearance of vastness.

I saw two naked people on the bed, one on top of the other, bare feet facing me. I thought they were tickling each other and when I giggled from the doorway, they both stopped moving and looked at me. The person on top was my mom's boyfriend and underneath him was Cinnamon. I was fixated by the sight of his penis inside her. When he had leaned slightly sideways to look at me, the pressure had caused one of her labia to flatten and I could see bulging veins in that bit of exposed skin. I looked up and saw Cinnamon's eyes resting on my face.

Her pleading eyes, didn't match her voice, 'Go out now sugar' she murmured.

So I did.

I never told my mom, I didn't know there was anything wrong with what they were doing. Sex to me was a natural part of life that I had glimpsed many people enjoying already in my short life. I assumed adults were expected to share everything too!

Cinnamon and my mom's boyfriend obviously were looking at the situation from an adult perspective and must have thought I would tell her what I had seen. As soon as she returned, they told her, arms crossed, voices muted, chins pointing down; standing before her like disobedient children. This confession escalated into a huge fight between my mother and her boyfriend. I leaped onto his back shrieking at him to stop shouting at my mom, to stop making her sad. I couldn't bear to see her cry, it both frightened me and made me senseless with rage.

Cinnamon stood in a corner, silent and pale, lips pressed tightly together. He flung me off him and I dropped to the wooden floor with a thud. My mother went to throw some of our things into a suitcase and then carried it and me out of the front door. She looked at the bedroom as she passed and said ' Huh! The nerve!'

We reached the bottom of the stairs before we heard him call her name. He was standing at the top of the wrought ion stair case and when we turned to look up at him, he began throwing arm loads of her clothes at us. They seemed to float momentarily in the air, like heavy petals, before landing on the stairs with a 'whap'! He filled the doorway, a fierce silhouette, arms akimbo on his hips. I could see Cinnamon looking over his shoulder. Her pale tear streaked cheeks glowed on one side from the street lights shinning in through the bedroom window.

Cinnamon saves Chewie doll

My mom's boyfriend moved out that weekend and we moved back in. It was my mom's apartment after all, the one she shared with my aunt and cousin and he knew better than to challenge a determined collective of them and their liberated friends. Those times being what they were, all about peace and free love supposedly, encouraged them to put aside their past and remain amicable; a good lesson that I practice to this day.

Cinnamon remained part of our circle. She was quite young, still a teenager though only just and was indulged by the circle of friends like a pampered and badly behaved child. She continued to occasionally dabble with other's partners, the men as well as the women. Again I thought nothing of this, although I was aware she was sexually active with both sexes, I had been raised to believe that we as hippies were 'recreating the rules' and therefore accepted differences in others without so much as a raised eyebrow of curiosity. Cinnamon remained unsatisfied, always seeking that extra thrill, which I suppose is why she became a runaway hippie in the first place.

Soon after we moved back in, the first snow of the year fell, 2 feet in a few hours! The very next day we went tobogganing with my cousin while my aunt was at work. This was just the greatest, most exhilarating experience ever and well worth the long trudge up the hill. My cousin and I trailed behind mom who was pulling the toboggan.

'Momeeee? Why can't we ride up on the babbogin?'

'Cos you are too heavy! Lets have a race and who ever gets up the hill first can sit at the front on the way down!'

'Yeaaaaahhhh!'

'Hee, hee, hee, hee, hee, OUCH, you meany poo poo!'

Frantic huffing uphill ensued as my cousin and I, ever competitive, slipped and slid and elbowed each other, in our haste to be the first to reach the summit. My mom slyly lagging behind, knowing she had to sit in the back so she could wrap her legs over both us and in that way make sure we didn't topple off at speed. We carried on in this way for hours, down the hill at great speed and back up the hill in a manner reminiscent of a tiny herd of turtles.

All too soon for us girls, it was time to go home, we were cold and Mom had to go to work. A warm bubble bath worked wonders as did the cup of hot chocolate that were got to drink with our lunch. My cousin, younger than me by a couple of years, fell asleep on the couch as I read to her. Soon after this Cinnamon arrived to look after me while my Mom went to work and also my cousin until my aunt had finished.

Later that afternoon, after my aunt had returned from work, Cinnamon took me out visiting with her. She loved to pretend that I was her little girl and would make up elaborate stories about her life as a single mother to people who stopped to comment on my platinum curls or dimples in my cheeks. People seemed much friendlier in those days and it was not at all unusual for strangers to strike up conversations in the shops, park or on the sidewalks.

On this day we went on our way to visit Sureety. She was having a party and we could hear the music from the end of the block. The door was unlocked and we entered without knocking, parting the haze of pot smoke before us like an uneven, double layered, 'Moses and the Red Sea' type of stunt. Cinnamon settled onto the couch, half on the lap of a man she wanted to 'get to know better' and I wandered off with my friend Christopher. His parents were at the party too and well known for their love of nudism. Soon everyone had their clothes off including us kids. We spent time playing with the cat and making a fort out of whatever materials we could find which included an open umbrella, the edge of a bed and several towels.

Except for an interruption from one adult we were left to our own devices. We played for a long time, cocooned in the dark womb of our fort, creating elaborate lives for ourselves. When we finally bored with our parallel world, the beat of the music seemed to be calling us and we emerged from our fort. We noticed familiar flashes coming from the noisy, fragrant smoke filled living room. Heading that way we were suddenly shy, lingering by the door and peeping in until someone noticed us.

'Hey kids! Get in here and have your picture taken!' shouted a man with a familiar face but whose name we did not know.

Feeling very uncomfortable, I held my Chewie doll over my pubic bone and hung back, shaking my head and looking anxiously around for Cinnamon as Christopher ran in to join them. The man walked over and snatched my Chewie doll from me, retreating and shaking her enticingly in my direction. I began to cry.

The bathroom door opened and Cinnamon came up behind me. Picking me up in her arms and cradling me like a baby, she took me into the bedroom where I had left my clothes. As she dressed me she muttered quietly.

'Did the man with the camera do anything to you just now?'

'He shouted at me, he took Chewie doll!'

'Did he touch you?'

'Ugh no, just poor Chewie, I want my Chewie!'

Cinnamon finished dressing me and then stomped off into the living room, holding my hand.

'Give me the doll right now!'

He shook his head and she reached out to try and snatch my Chewie doll, anger blazed across her delicate, speckled egg shell features.

'Better give it to her man' a voice, raised slightly in the first key of 'angry', floated from the depths of that murky room.

Fumbling with anger, he threw my soft bit of comfort in her direction, making sure to toss gently enough that it fell short of her and she had to stoop to pick it up. She handed it to me and I clutched Chewie to my cheek with one hand, thumb of the other plugged firmly into my mouth, frantically sucking familiar comfort. Chewie had the face of a Kewpie doll and was covered in soft green fabric which came to a peak at the top, opening around her face. A little yellow kiss curl had been moulded onto her forehead. I loved to hold the fuzzy green peak and rub it against my face. Thinking of it even now makes me want to suck my thumb in an attempt to recreate those soothing endorphin surges.

We left, with me bundled up against the cold in an all in one snow suit. My cheeks flamed in the cold, my breath pluming before me, like a cleaner version of the cloud in the room we had left.

Cinnamon said, 'You feeling happier now sugar?'

When I nodded, she said, 'This will be our secret okay? You don't need to tell your mom how well I took care of you and protected you and Chewie from that bad man. I would just get embarrassed...you don't want me to feel like that do you?'

I shook my head.

I didn't tell my mom about Cinnamon saving Chewie doll. Nor did I tell my Mom or Cinnamon about the man taking pictures of Christopher and me, naked, unsupervised and vulnerable in our umbrella fort.

The wooden pickle barrel

There was a shop at the end of our street. It was a long narrow rectangle of a room, shelves to the left and display cases to the right, with wooden floors that moaned with the pressure of each foot step. The premises were always dimly lit as the shop window was all but obscured by the hanging displays of cheese and sausage. The owner seemed to have a fondness for low wattage light bulbs, although this could have been an illusion caused by shadows thrown from the cured meats, dried herbs and spices which hung from ceiling racks.

I am sure he knew how poor we were as he would often beckon my mother and I to come inside as we were passing. He would have some soup bones wrapped in butcher's paper ready to press firmly into my Mom's hands, ignoring her pretence at protest. More intent on the treasure in the far rear right hand corner, I never paid much attention to them or the various jars of sweets on the counter or what hung above my direct line of vision. The object of my desire was the huge wooden pickle barrel. The owner would always offer me a lollipop, his cheeks apple shaped with mirth as he laughed at my firmly shaken head and tight lipped 'no thank you'.

I hated being teased and knew that he was fully aware of what I really wanted him to offer me. He always spun out the suspense, and when this was experienced by my 4 year old psyche, it seemed to be at my prides' expense. In hindsight I now realise that he probably prolonged those moments in order to fully to enjoy the escape granted by being able to share a laugh with a pretty woman, whose daughter's curls would bounce as she shook her head in temper. Eventually he would put the lollipop back in the jar and gesture towards the stained brown barrel in the far corner.

'Go child, chose your zaftig pickle.'

I knew from previous questioning that 'zaftig' meant, plump and juicy. I would walk slowly away from them, trying to convince them that I wasn't ecstatic at being granted my wish and not so secretly thrilled that each step was bringing me closer to the barrel full of pickled treats. The smell of the brine grew stronger with each step and my mouth would be watering by the time I was within arms reach of the steel banded, salt marked wood. Nestled against the back was an ancient wooden milking stool, it's horsehair stuffing bursting through in places from the leather covered seat. I was always a stickler for adhering to ritual and each time I used to mount this stool, in order to be able to look down upon the pickles bobbing in the salt, spice and vinegar bath. I would examine each pickle that I could see on or near the surface before grasping my prize.

The sign on the barrel said 1 for 3 cents or 2 for 5 cents but I don't remember any money ever changing hands and my mother would not have been able to afford to indulge me in this regular expense. The photos I have from that age show a woman with long flowing skirts, a generous smile, a shining sheet of dark hair and a rippling aura of sensuality. The combination of these assets must have made precious moments with her worth the expense of the occasional free pickle, if it kept her daughter and therefore her happy. With the pickle clutched firmly in my pudgy 4 year old hand, we would step out the door and blink away the temporary blindness induced by the brightness outside the shop. Then with unencumbered hands clasped, we would make our way onto wherever we had been headed before being beckoned into the shop full of laughter and pickles.

A higher state of consciousness

'Hare Krishna Hare Krishna, Krishna Krishna Hare Hare, Hare Rama Hare Rama, Rama Rama Hare Hare'.

The men flowed around, chanting their mantra, with orange robes swirling in a hypnotic rhythm. To my four year old eyes it was an expression of joy and my ears did not disagree with this interpretation. I clutched my mother's hand, leaning eagerly towards the spectacle on the street. I wanted to leap into their midst and dance with utter abandon too!

We had just come down from the playground on the high hill in the nearby park. The sugar maples' leaves coated the ground in contrasting reds and oranges and I had 3 of the finest I had been able to find clutched in my fist. I shook these in time to the chanting, a gleeful grin on my face. One of the men broke away from the group and began to circulate the crowd, distributing leaflets to those who would accept. He approached us and I lifted a glowing orange leaf and offered it to him. Crouching down he smiled and spoke.
'You like pretty colours little lady?'
Suddenly and uncharacteristically shy, I could only nod in response, now clinging to my mother's leg.
'You are welcome to join us at our feast tonight in the Temple.'

My mother always one to indulge in new experiences and immerse me in the experience of other cultures, accepted his offer. He gave her directions to the Temple, looking up at her as he was still crouched at my level and then once again focused his attention on me.

'You will enjoy our food I think... many, many colours for you to taste." He shook his tambourine and whirled away like a magical orange spirit.

The Temple tables were laden with rows of brightly coloured foods. I was captivated by the lushness spread before me. I do not remember where we sat to enjoy this vegetarian feast, nor what I chose from the main course dishes but I will never forget the taste of the sweets I ate that night. My particular favourite was a firm paste squeezed from sesame seeds and pressed into a solid cake, called Halva. It broke off in large flakes of moist deliciousness that melted in my mouth.

I floated home that night, moving my feet without any sensation of the pavement under them. I was ecstatic from the stimulation of all those colours and new flavours. They still burn brightly for me to this day.

'Plashing in puddles

To the passers-by my cousin and I must have looked like a cartoonist's sketch of alternate sides of a film strip negative. She was all sun kissed sepia tone skin and huge brown eyes. I was cream coloured with eyes that my mother said had to have come from the aliens because they were impossibly big and blue-hazel coloured. Both of us were graced with eyelashes that fanned our cheeks when we shut our eyes. Her curls were delightful dark chocolate springs that bounced and jostled and mine were looser coils of shimmering platinum.

We shared a fiery temper that made a mockery of our indulged childhoods. By indulged, I do not mean we were spoiled, at least not in terms of wealth and material possessions, though I suppose we were spoiled in relation to the amount of love bestowed upon us by familiar adults. Our mothers lived together and the two of us, so similar in many ways, fought with the viciousness particular to children and psychotics. Even today, though we are no longer children and definitely not psychotic (that is my opinion and I am sticking to it!); we still are not friends.

On that day and much to our mothers' relief, we were enjoying a rare moment of camaraderie, laughing and playing with gusto. It had been raining hard earlier in the day and our mothers had decided on a trip to the library to wile away a rainy day. By the time we left the library, the rain had stopped leaving steaming sidewalks and patches of gleaming puddles.

My cousin and I, wearing rain boots, stomped and splashed our way through any puddles we could find. Ever competitive, we aimed each splash in the other's direction. Soon we were thoroughly soaked and ended up sitting in a deep puddle and whooshing water over each other. Our mothers huddled against each other, dodging stray droplets and laughing vigorously.

A group of older women who were passing, tutted disapprovingly. One of them stopped; towering over our tiny forms and said with a frown

'Is that any way for little ladies to behave?

Whatever are you two playing at?'

Emboldened by my cousins complicity in this mess and my mothers' protective presence, I boldly shouted 'We are 'plashing in puddles big lady!'

Our mothers shrieked with laughter and hauled us out of the muddy puddle. 'Come on girls, time to go home for a very hot bath'. I am reliably informed that the gleeful playing in water continued that afternoon in the comfort of our home.

Lucky Girl

'Lucky girl!'

Those were the words my mother said and always with an audible exclamation mark, each time she put food in front of me. With those 2 words she wove a spell that never failed to convince me that I would enjoy whatever was on my plate, even if it was new to my uneducated palate. In my short life to date, I had been encouraged to sample and enjoy choice dishes which formed a vast and varied diet from all the food groups and many different cultures. There was only one substance so despicable that even her magic couldn't convince me to taste it after the first time, tomatoes! Urgh, unless they were blended into to a sauce, the texture made me shudder.

I occasionally had to be looked after by a child minder as we had not yet moved to the same Province as my Aunt and cousin. Usually, if this was necessary, I was taken care of by friends of my mother; fellow hippies who were relaxed, probably stoned and happy to spend time indulging me by answering my endless questions about everything. On rare occasions when friends were not available, my mother would pay for a child minder to come and care for me. This woman was not a hippy, she was of some Eastern European descent and firmly believed that children should be seen but not heard! So she would keep a close eye on me, but would not show any tenderness towards me and refused to answer any of my questions.

'You wait und asx ur movver ewe noisy child!' was her routine reply to any question put to her in my piping bird-like pitch.

Her arms braced on her knees to prevent me climbing onto her lap in search of a little emotional warmth and comfort. She did indeed look after me in my mothers' absence but she did not love me and this was a disturbing sensation, for I had always been showered with loving attention by the adults tasked with caring for me.

I would watch her shaking her head at the wild profusion of fabrics which were draped over our chairs, falling in lush folds from curtain rails and folded on the couch. Rich green foliage breathed life into this organised chaos, hanging from homemade macramé hangers, with beads and shells cleverly wound into the pattern of the plant holder. Many inspirational and beautiful works of art adorned the walls of our cosy home, trailing ferns shadowing shelves which bulged with a well thumbed assortment. A delightful flowering arrangement added their charm; placed just so on a rickety wooden ladder painted with various peaceful and harmonious symbols. My mother's creative skills also served to disguise the tatty woodwork, various holes left in anger by previous tenants and stains from the landlords' twice yearly cockroach fumigations.

I was astonished that she could look round our house and find it lacking for I thought it wonderful beyond all imagining, rich with vibrant colours, delightful art and luxuriant foliage. Just the thing to nurture a healthy inquisitive child's mind and to generate countless questions! On one occasion I had to go to this woman's house to be looked after as my mother had to go somewhere at short notice. She could not come to our house as she was already looking after her niece and nephew. I only remember one experience from that time in her house.

We were sat at the cold Formica covered dinner table, the niece and nephew on one side and me facing them, my slippery chair seat too low to boost me up to a comfortable level when eating. When the steaming bowl of food was placed in front of me, I knew my life had just become very difficult. Inside the bowl were what looked to my 3 year old eyes like watery noodles with stewed tomatoes sitting on top. Now I knew that there was no way I would eat those tomatoes! I was a good girl, loved food and was keen to please adults, but tomatoes brought out my latent non-compliance. However I also knew that there was no way this stern woman would allow me to turn my nose up at her food and leave the table with the food uneaten.

I watched, horrified, as her niece and nephew tucked into their bowls, surely no one actually enjoyed food that looked as bland as this and which was topped with tomatoes?!

They waited till their aunt turned her back to us and continued her clattering at the stove and then they whispered to me, 'Just swallow it without chewing, that's what we do!'

I took a single piece of the pasta onto my spoon, took a deep breath and popped it into my mouth and swallowed. The tomato taste rose sickeningly up my throat and I had to fight to keep the food in my stomach. I began to cry knowing I would not be able to finish that bowl of food.

Turning back from the stove with a laden bowl of her own, she saw me crying and guessing the reason why, snapped out, 'Ewe are a spoilt ungrateful child und ewe will sit there until you have done eating what has been given before you!'

Sit there I did, humiliated beyond belief as her niece and nephew tucked into their dessert and then were excused to go play. Tears rolled down my cheeks, dropping into my bowl and mixing with the liquid already present. I cried and watched the mixture swirling around in iridescent patterns until my mother arrived.

'What is going on?! Why is she crying?', she said to the woman.

'Why are you crying?, she asked me; panic, anger and fear combining to make her eyes appear luminescent as I looked at her through my wet lashes.

Spotting the tomatoes in my bowl as she scooped me up and held me close, she said 'Didn't you tell her that you don't like tomatoes?', confusion clear in her tone.

Lips trembling, eyes brimming with tears, I nodded and then hid my face in her neck. I could sense my mothers' unhappiness and smell her rage when she realised that this woman had treated me as if I was an insect or some other life form unable to voice a personal choice. This was unacceptable in my mother's world of peace where the freedom to love without exception was the only expectation. Needless to say, I was never looked after by that woman again. I considered myself a very lucky girl after that...

The candy tree forest

I was snuggled down into my nest in the back seat of the car. I always made one up for long trips, placing my pillows against the right hand side door and my blanket puddled around my legs. From this vantage point I could see the side of my moms' face as she drove and I would fluctuate between constant chatter and sleep, thumb plugged in my mouth and my 'chewie' doll within arms reach. In those days it was easy to stretch out and get comfortable as seat belt laws hadn't been invented yet and that meant the whole seat was available for use as a bed.

It was mid February and cold outside, snow piled in high banks on top of the ditches that lined the bumpy gravel road. The breeze that seeped in from the open quarter panel window felt like icy fingers when it reached by my face. I turned to the window and watched the smoke from my mom's friend's spliff drift outside, dance around and disappear. He smoked it slowly, joint pinched between his forefinger and thumb, inhaling deeply, holding his breath for many heartbeats before exhaling. Occasionally he would tilt his hand to the left in case my mom felt like indulging. She would shake her head each time, never willing to take her hands from the steering wheel, carefully following the packed snow trail laid down by previous cars tires. I mimicked his actions, breathing in deeply and trying to draw some of its sweet scent back towards me.

I loved the smell of marijuana and everything that it signified to my 4 year old brain. It still evokes feelings of security for me, of peaceful happy childhood moments surrounded by clusters of chatting, smiling, dreamy adults.

When I first encountered a group of drunk adults at the age of nine, I was terrified by their violent and aggressive manner and completely unprepared for the effect other intoxicants could have on people.

That cold day we were driving my mom's friend to the sugar maple farm so he could help with tapping the trees in order to collect the sap that would soon start running. Maple sugar season was here and mom said we would stay for the weekend. I loved the farmhouse with its huge wood stove, the stew pot was always full of fragrant contents, big lumpy beds with thick handmade quilts and goofy working dogs who delighted in the attention I lavished on them. The owner of these dogs and the farm was a pleasant mixture of warm crinkly smiles and wild frizzy grey hair; her wide hips and an ample bosom adding to my impression of a stereotypical fairy godmother. I loved her dearly and called her my 'sugar plump fairy', but what I meant was that she was like the Christmas 'sugar plum fairy'. Except greyer...a lot greyer!

The next day we were up early, I was dressed in so many layers of thick clothing that it was impossible to press my arms flat against my sides. This was not a problem as it meant I was warm and I had absolutely no intention of keeping my arms still anyway! We rode out to the maple forest on a sleigh which was drawn by a single huge Clydesdale horse. His hooves were the size of my head but he had the gentlest soul and was always willing to have me placed upon his back. He would walk gently around while I chirped in my shrill bird song pitched voice, exhilarated and running a constant commentary on all the things I could see from the great height I had attained.

On this day, the sleigh he pulled was loaded with taps and some drills. Up to three taps per tree would be inserted once the holes had been drilled. I spent the day playing with the goofy dogs, stroking the horse, his coarse hair making my hands grubby and generally making a nuisance of myself. I would alternate between standing back and observing the work taking place while chattering away and getting way too close while the taps were pounded into the trees. Eventually the sugar plump fairy pulled me aside.

'Do you know where we are?', she filled my field of vision as she stood before me, hands shoved in her pockets.

I giggled and waved my hand over my head, gesturing at the trees all around us. 'The maple tree farm, silly!'

'Ah yes but I know a special secret about this place... I will whisper it to you...'

She leaned towards me, her lips tickling my ear and her wiry hair pressed into the side of my face. 'This is the candy tree forest and the trees have asked me to give you something and to tell you it tastes best if you let it melt in your mouth with your eyes shut... She paused and drew her head back to look me in the eyes... Do you think you can do that?'

I nodded eagerly, climbing up onto the sleigh and shutting my eyes. I felt her press something with the texture of a sugar lump into my palm. I held it between my fingers, lifted my hand and took a bite. As it began to melt on my tongue, my mouth was flooded with the sweetness of maple sugar candy and my imagination thrilled with the magic of this gift from the candy trees.

A special treat

Our little room was bright, all the shadows had gone. The plant leaves appeared transparent, green veins highlighted by the sun shine. Hung beside the window, bleached by exposure to the sun, was a white rope of braided garlic. I had spotted it and many others draped over the handle bars of a bicycle at a farmers market. Entranced by this sight I had begged my mother to buy one.

It was now a little tatty as my mother frequently removed cloves from their papery wraps to add to our meals. Blending in with the garlic rope was the cord which anchored the drying rack to a hook in the window frame. It was currently up near the ceiling, making the most of the rising warmth; heavy with the weight of drying bananas, apples, figs, plums and various medicinal herbs.

My mother was training to become a chartered herbalist and we were enjoying daily expeditions to look for herbal treasures to bring home. Yarrow, dandelion and clover were available from the parks in our city and marigold, mint and rose hips were abundant in gardens left to grow wild through the neglect of some of my mother's friends.

'Crunch, crush, grind, scrape' the coffee beans seemed to say as they were ground to a coarse texture under moms' pestle in the kitchen on this fine day, the smell of drying mint a subtle undertone to the more bitter scent of the caffeine laden blend.

I used my stool to reach into the cupboards and one by one, took out the things we would need for our breakfast.

Croissants, rose hip jam, butter and honey. Plates and cups; the bone china one for mom, held tight against my chest as I carried it to the table and a sturdy clay mug with a silly face on it for me. From the fridge I removed the cream, which mom used to sweeten her coffee. A jug carved from driftwood, grey with age, contained the cutlery and I placed it on the table along with everything else I had gathered.

'All ready?' she sang as she opened the oven door and removed the warmed croissants.

I nodded when she looked at me, holding her book and mine.

'Sit down then, I've made you a special treat!'

She placed a cup of milky hot chocolate in front of me. I looked in, breath held and then released in a rush of happiness as I spotted the tiny marshmallows floating on the surface.

I copied her actions as she tore off bits of warm, flaky pastry and dunked them in her cup. The combination of buttery bites and sweet chocolate was delightful. My mom read while she ate, book held open by bracing the pages on one side with her thumb, spine balanced on her middle 3 fingers and other side pinned down by her baby finger. I had yet to master this trick!

When I had finished my mother was still eating, out of habit she was contentedly chewing each bite more times than necessary, and deeply absorbed in her book. I placed my plate in the sink, opened my book in its place on the table and read with my head propped up on my hands. The wood of the table was warm under my elbows. I was vaguely aware of feeling loved, secure and settled and of my soul swelling with contentment.

The pinwheel lollipop

The day began with the realisation that my mother was still not home from her night out. At that time, I thought this was outrageous! In actuality it was not yet 8am and I was safe with my grandmother so it wasn't really shocking behaviour. However, I was only 3 1/2, unable to tell time and still very egocentric. Now that I am in my 40's, I can understand why she wanted a night out! She was a young woman, single and lucky enough to be part of the generation striving for peace and free love.

I had slept cosily in my crib, nestled amongst so many toys that there was hardly any mattress space for me. I didn't mind as I loved to lie on top of my soft toys, neck supported by a teddy's belly, head pillowed on a smiling sunflower, outstretched arm covering a fluffy doggy, hand clutching my Chewie doll and other hand's thumb plugged in my mouth.

Upon waking I had stood up looking for my mother's sleeping form on the metal framed bed beside my cosy nest. Flat bed covers and empty pillows equalled no mom and I began to squall, frightening my grandmother into hurrying from her peaceful morning coffee into my room.

'Curly girlie! There no need to cry! What ever is the matter with you? Did you have a bad dream?' She stood before me, arms on her hips, assessing the situation, looking for damage to my body.

'Muuumeeee....?' Pointing past my grandmother towards the open door, anxiously hopeful.

'She won't be long! Now stop fretting and come have some breakfast with your grammie.' Her tone of voice implying that my mother had better be home soon if she ever wanted another child free night out. She looked at my wild, curly and somewhat matted hair; tsk'd and took down the hairbrush.

'I can do it myself grammie... mommy lets me!' I cringed away from the hair brush which I knew would hurt, raising my hands in an attempt to bat hers away.

Lifting up a section at the back she said despairingly; 'If you can do it then why is your hair all matted here?'

'Mommy lets me lets me do it myself!' (I firmly believed that the best solution for unanswerable questions lay in deflecting them with repetition of a statement until the questioner admitted defeat!) I was very proud of brushing my own hair and spent considerable time slicking the brush over the top surface till it gleamed, fooling both myself and my mother into believing I had done a thorough job of it. My theory didn't work on grammie and I grimly endured a brushing which made my eyes water. She finished the job by fastening my hair into a style which she felt more suitable than my usual 'bed head' look.

We ate together at her table in the kitchen; the hair grips made my hair feel tight. Slimy, slightly salty tasting porridge with plump raisins for me, homemade English muffins for her. From my seat I had a view of her living room, the sun shone in through the window bleaching her carpet. Dust motes floated in the air as if hesitant to alight on the shinny surfaces of grammie's gleaming woodwork. Her bird, Huxley, hopped from perch to cage bottom and back up again. He alternately pulled at the bars of his cage with his beak and pecked at the plastic bird tied to his perch, an uninvited and unwelcome presence which he did not want in his already miniature territory. Aggressively he would batter the tiny bell tied to his ladder, back and forth, back and forth his beak would swipe across the shiny surface. Seeming angry when the bell swung in rhythm with it's clapper so no sound emerged, he would fling his bird seed onto the carpet below before plucking a few feathers from his shoulders which would float softly down to join the others.

It made me feel sad to watch him but watch I did with the innate fascination humans have for observing others in crisis. Survival of the fittest; watch these actions, learn from them, do not do this and so on... Displaying the slightly insane, agitated wanderings of a wild soul unnaturally caged. I was just beginning to make conscious attempts at rationalisation and seeing the distress her bird was in, I decided that my grandmother did not love him! My mother often told me (usually when I was trying to capture one of my current obsessions, ladybirds and butterflies), that all living things had a right to be free, even ones that we really loved and wanted to keep close to us. I knew that if mom said so then this must be true but I did wonder why she had not yet told my grammie. Maybe if grammie knew then she would let her bird go free.

During our breakfast, I constantly twisted round in my chair to stare at the front door, willing it to open, until my grandmother gave up hope of me finishing my forgotten, congealed bowl of food.

'Down you get, you can take a vitamin instead to replace the goodness you missed out on.'

I stood by the sink watching her take down the bottle, expecting the liquid I was used to but instead being handed a little red pill. Confused, I held it in my hand and frowned. My grandmother 'tsk'd' to herself, took the pill back from me and placing it in a teaspoon, crushed it with the pressure of another spoon on top. Then she mixed it with a dab of honey and gave it to me to eat off the spoon.

Not a word was spoken during this preparation and in that short time, my senses tipped into over stimulation, heightening my awareness of everything. I could hear the fluorescent lights buzzing, smell the coffee on the stove, smell the bleach that the dish cloth was soaking in, and hear her bird rustling around in its cage but most of all I could smell the bitterness of the vitamin not quite masked by the sweetness of the honey disguise. Held my breath, opened my mouth, tipped the spoon upside down, pulled it off the spoon with my tongue curled up over itself (best way to avoid tasting yucky things) and swallowed.

'Good girl! Tomorrow if you don't finish your breakfast, I will teach you how to swallow the vitamin whole!' No smile punctuated this sentence and I decided there and then I would eat fast enough to finish my breakfast tomorrow.

When my mother returned home, I followed her around not letting her out of my sight until she escaped by going to soak in the bath. I loitered in the corridor, chattering to her through the door until she told me to go into my aunt's room and look for dolls to play with. I found this prospect quite exciting as I only had soft toys. I loved the thought of being allowed into this room which was normally off limits when my aunt was at school and the grown- upness of playing with her dolls.

'Oka -ay!' I shouted over my shoulder as I ran the few steps to her room and barged in eagerly.

The room was very tidy, items lined up on shelves as if on display for sale. I cast my eyes curiously over this room, doll hunt forgotten as I spied a pinwheel lollipop. I grabbed it and knowing my mother would never agree to allow me such a sugar laden treat, I went in search of my grandmother. I was getting the hang of this rationalisation business and had correctly assumed that if my aunt had it in her room then my grandmother sanctioned the consumption of such delights.

'Grammie... look what I found!'

'Oh found it did you? Where might I ask?!'

'In Auntie Marg's room, Mommy said I could go in...'

'Well I think you'd better ask her if you can share it with her when she gets home from school because it is hers and not mine to give away.'

'Okay...' eyes on floor, disappointed, hoping but not believing my aunt would say yes, I gave my grammie the lollipop and she placed it up high out of my reach. Her words and tone had been harsh but the hug she gave me then beautifully conveyed all her latent love. I spent most of the day loitering nearby, my longed for candy safe on it's self, my eyes lingering on the door and my heart longing for my aunt to walk in!

Eventually she did and I leapt on her, talking nonsense in my excitement.

She laughed. 'I bought it ages ago and forgot all about eating it, you must have been the reason why!'

Holding me tight, propped on her skinny hip, she walked over to where I pointed, taking the pinwheel down and handing it to me. This memory is one of the reasons that I am convinced that children remember kindnesses bestowed upon them, even ones that may seem insignificant to adult.

'They're not just spoons, petit minou' (Little cat/kitten)

Writing about visiting my grammie reminded me of the time when I was 6 or 7 and we went to Prince Edward Island (PEI), where my grampie lived. PEI is a really unique colour, the whole island rooted in soil the colour of brick dust. grampie said it was a reflection of it's high iron content. After he had told me this, I knelt on the seat and watched the passing scenery from the rear windscreen, trying to spot the irons.

'Whatchu duin mon petit?' (My little one) His mixture of Quebecquois French and Canadian perfectly showcased his heritage, which was known as French Matis, a blend of Canadian Indian and Canadian French Caucasian.
'Looking for the irons in the dirt grampie'.
From the front seat came an almost palpable pause, a puzzled glance between my mother and him and then his deep laugh rumbled over the seat towards me.
'Mais non! (But no!) Not irons for clothes! Iron which is sort of like a powder called iron oxide. Just like old metal rusts when it gets touched by rain, cold and sunshine, the iron in this soil does the same when it gets touched by air.'
I was deep in thought, what we call an 'Arsenault trance' and did not comment when he finished speaking.
'Eh?' he prompted me, seeking a response to his explanation.
'Oh!' and at that moment, the birth of my love for chemistry was witnessed by my mother as she watched my eyes brighten with understanding.

We passed miles upon miles of potato fields, the

blackish green of the plants a stark contrast to the deep orange soil. Even the dust that billowed from the dirt road under the car was the colour of pumpkins and seemed as if it was trying to reach the sky so it could join the colours of the sunset.

We had just finished eating a mess of fresh lobster for our supper and I was playing with a claw, making it clack shut and spring open; the lobster juices beginning to sting my fingers . My mom was in the kitchen making coffee and dishing up our dessert. Grampie sat at the table watching and encouraging me to listen to the logs crackling in the fireplace.

He explained that the burning of the logs was a chemical process similar to the iron changing the colour of the dirt.
'The logs are hard and then, the fire, pooof(!), it changes them into heat, charcoal and ash!'
In his excitement at imparting more knowledge to a mesmerised audience of one, this mini teaching session was accompanied by his hands gesturing exuberantly as he used them to accent and punctuate his words.

I stopped playing with the lobster claw and sat silently watching the fire. I was silently repeating his words, turning them around in my mind, looking at them from every angle while trying to absorb this knowledge. I had big plans to take this information back with me and wow my teacher with it! Occasionally the logs would hiss and spit an ember onto the floor. Eventually grampie got up and shoved the logs farther back into their pit.
Sitting back down he took his spoon and mine and securing them on either side of his thumb and forefinger he

began to rap them together, cupping his other hand and patting out a rhythm on his knee. I stood up.

'Grampie! Those are for eating with!' hands on hips, scowl on face, I scolded him. These adults, they sure got up to some strange things.

'Mais non, petit minou ('but no, little cat/kitten'), they are not just spoons!'

He stopped as we heard the back door open (no friend knocked if expected in those days and doors were never locked in small communities).

I heard my mom saying with a smile in her voice, 'Salut! Ca va?' (Hello! Okay? Are you well?*direct translation not possible*)

The replies came from several voices:
'Mais oui, et tu?' (Yes and you?)
'Bonsoir ma belle!' Good evening beautiful!)
'Ca va bien!' (I am good)
'Salut!' (Hello!)
'Ou est la petit et votre pere?' (Where are the little one and your father?).

'In front of the fire, I heard him warming up his spoons just now! Go through and I will bring coffee and desert for you.'

The youngest of grampie's friends stayed to help mom with her work in the kitchen and I could hear her giggling as he spoke. The rest of them came in carrying instruments which they told me were called, a banjo, a dulcimer, a mouth harp and an accordion. Once everyone was settled and had eaten their fill of mom's blackberry cobbler, they began to play. I cuddled up on mom's lap and drifted on the sound of the music. Grampie's spoons and the sound of the mouth harp carried their rhythmic notes to my ears ; murmuring to me under the weight of the other instruments' music as the fire danced in front of my drooping eye lids.

'Hands, Handkerchief, Thumbs'

I fell in love with reading books at the age of four. Not just being read books, I mean reading them myself! My mom said I spoke my first words at 10 months of age and was speaking in full sentences from a year old; perhaps I took to reading so young because I was running out of things to say? Many would disagree and say I haven't stopped talking since I started...I find it most effective to just ignore them and carry on with whatever conversation I happen to be having at the time!

The apartment we lived in had floor to ceiling windows, wrought iron railings ran across them up to my chest height on the outside. The wooden floor, polished till it gleamed and slippery as wet marble, was partly covered with a large Turkish rug. I was convinced that it was a magic carpet and would sit on it, legs crossed, holding onto the tassels and shouting 'Hey presto! Take me to Kalamazoo!', my imagination already carrying the carpet away on beds of fluffy clouds. Every so often I would feel it shift and eagerly anticipated a sudden rise up into the air. I later realised that the shift coincided with adults walking into the living room from the hallway behind me; their weight causing the floorboards to bounce. Gah! Reality can be so disappointing at times...

As always, I was eager to gain the approval of others and on this day was reading aloud to an audience of several adults. I lay on my stomach, elbows digging into the rug and my hands supporting my face. I remember struggling with a word in my Dr Seuss book. Forever imprinted on my mind is the line; 'Hands, Handkerchief, Thumb' because it was the word handkerchief that I struggling to form into a sound with meaning. It was worth the effort because when I managed to sound it out, all the adults clapped! I felt so proud of myself. I can not remember which Dr Seuss book it was, just that line from it. I remember insisting that I be allowed to read it to every person I encountered for months thereafter, the shop keepers, librarian, strangers in the park, anyone I could find! I would love to find the book now to read it once again and to enjoy watching my youngest learn to read it for himself.

Once my recital was complete, the circle of adults around me drifted off and I went to sit with Cinnamon. She was a runaway hippie teenager who had the good fortune to hook up with my mom's group. As I explained in Chapter 3, she would look after my cousin and me when my mom and auntie were at work. Eventually everyone left and my mom and aunt decided to make supper. The only problem was that there was not much food in the house and certainly not enough to make a protein rich dish which would feed two growing kids and their hungry mothers.

My mom and aunt went through the house searching for any spare money, checking pockets, and shelves, eventually finding several coins under the couch cushions. My aunt set off to the shops and returned with a chicken that proved to be quite stinky once the plastic wrap was removed! My mom and aunt started giggling which I thought was strange at the time but now understand must have been somewhat hysterical in nature.

'I guess that explains why it was so cheap!'

My aunt's sarcasm set them off into renewed gales of laughter until they had to crouch to keep from peeing themselves and were wiping the tears from their cheeks.

An option of eating bad smelling chicken or going without food for a couple of meals was not really a choice with two hungry children. My cousin and I stood on chairs and watched as they scrubbed out the kitchen sink and filled it with water to which they added lots of bleach. What a smell! My cousin and I held our noses and looked around our hands at each other. Whatever would our moms do next? That unspoken question was answered when the chicken went in for a vigorous scrub! Then the sink was drained and the chicken rinsed. A few suspicious sniffs and it was pronounced safe to cook.

They cooked it and we ate it. My cousin and I were too hungry and trusting to even worry about getting sick from it but I can imagine that my mom and aunt were less than delighted to be eating the foul fowl! The bleach laden bath must have done the trick as none of us suffered any ill effects.

Memory slide show

Today I was listening to my son ramble on about anything that took his fancy; peppering the monologue with liberal amounts of questions. He was completely oblivious to the participation, or otherwise, of his audience of one. Suddenly it dawned on me that other than the fact that he is a boy and as camp as a row of tents, I appear to have given birth to a clone. All his odd ways are mirrored in my memories of things I did as a child. I catch people looking at him with a puzzled expression on their face and wonder what reactions I must have provoked at the same age.

Lulled by his early morning monologue, my mind drifted, flashing through a series of random snap shot memories. I used to eat some strange things as a child and having a fair amount of freedom meant I got the opportunity to indulge my appetite. The memories that spring most readily to mind are: eating burnt toast from a garbage bag, pulling burnt match heads with my teeth off the stick and into my mouth and brushing the lint off a drop candy I found under a bench and savouring every bit of sweetness till it had melted away. I mourned the end of that flavour. For some reason I remember being aware that picking up the candy and eating it was wrong (not that it stopped me) but not with the former two items.

By the time I was 6, we lived in the French speaking part of Canada and although it was my second language, all my friends spoke French as their first language with very little if any English. I chose to go to a French speaking Catholic school because that was where my friends attended.

I wasn't prepared for the nuns and nor were they for me and my wild ways!

My mother would not allow them to make me join in on the prayer sessions, instead I sat and stared at my classmates, their heads bent piously in prayer. Thankfully, I did not have to wear a uniform. I much preferred my eclectic dress sense with usually meant wearing 2 skirts in contrasting colours at the same time by layering them onto on each other.

For show and tell other children brought in family pets, pictures of their younger siblings, stories about their family vacations or family bibles: I brought in a beaded, macrame'd plant hanger made from hemp twine and crafted by my mother. The nuns were not too thrilled when I explained the origins of hemp to the class.

One winter the school caretaker built us an ice castle! It got very cold in this part of Canada and he blocked off our access to the playground equipments and begin spraying water over it from late October. The water froze, stayed frozen and over a period of a week or two, a magical shimmering ice fort grew before our expectant eyes as he built it up in daily layers.

He began to add plastic tunnels to the structure, sticking them on with a film of near frozen water and then covered in freezing layers till tunnels began to form. We would gather around the barrier at recess, watching it and hoping that this would be the day we'd be allowed to play. The day we saw him breaking apart and removing the plastic inside the ice tunnel and cutting in a set of steps with his axe, we knew our wait was almost over. We were silent as we watched the ice chips fly from the axe blade; mesmerised by the way they caught the sunshine and flew through the air like thousands of mini rainbows, turning the scene into a living prism.

The very next day we got to explore this magical structure. Wrapped snugly in our all in one snow suits we clambered around, peeping at each other through holes that had been chopped into the ice, crawling through short tunnels and whizzing down the slide, skidding along the long horizontal ice path until we came to a gentle stop against the snow drift at the end.

The most amazing, surreal part of the day was the row of nuns dressed in their dull grey cloaks and the priest in his long gleaming black Franciscan robes, lined up where the barriers used to be. They were watching us, smiling, cheering and clapping their hands at our antics. I suspect nowadays such a structure wouldn't even be allowed due to 'health and safety' rules but I don't remember anyone ever getting hurt.

Stranded

'It hurts!' I shrieked.

'It hurts mee so baaaaad!' I wailed, pounding my fists on the man in front of me

My words trailed off into inaudible sobs. The snow was being driven into my exposed skin like millions of cold needles and the wind was roaring as it whipped itself into a frenzy. The man in front (my brother's father), was doing his best to shield me, as was my mother behind. The wind was not fooled and it forced the snowflakes into weapons which it hurled with malevolent fury.

I was terrified...

We were on our way to collect my brother from the hospital in late October when the blizzard hit unexpectedly. He was just 4 months old and had been suffering from severe bronchitis. I knew he was ill when I could hear him breathing in the night, his room was at the opposite end of the corridor from mine, but I was still so shocked when he was admitted to hospital. His face looked so small with the oxygen mask on. I thought people went to hospitals to die. In 4 short months I had forgotten there used to be a world without my brother in it. I hung around him trying to make him laugh because when he did the air around him seemed to sparkle. Mom said it was his magic, the magical powers of love.

The night of the blizzard, I was a few months into my 9th year and certain that I was about to die. If not from cold, or fear, then from the worry of how we would get to the safety and warmth of the articulated 18 wheeler. It was slightly ahead of us and just visible where it was parked with its lights flashing, on the other side of the road. So paralysed by these things that I could not move even one step more, even if it meant we would be warm, safe and able to bring the magic of my brother home.

My brothers' father stopped so suddenly that my mothers' momentum pushed me into his back with enough force that I then dropped to the ground. He turned and gathered me roughly into his arms, my face shielded against his coat. At the time I thought he was protecting me but age tells me he was more likely to have been angry with me for my antics in such a dangerous situation. Nevertheless, he wrapped his arms securely around me and they warmed me where they rested on my thinner coat. I had refused to wear my dark green winter coat and insisted I would only wear my pretty red and black tartan patterned coat. It was wool but not warm enough for a blizzard. I wanted to look interesting for my brother; to give him cause to laugh with delight at the colours of my coat and to watch him reach out to grasp the wooden peg buttons in his pudgy hands.

They fought their way across the road, him carrying me and my mother clutching onto his coat tail so that we would not get separated. As we approached the cab of the big rig, the door opened slightly and then all the way as the wind took it in a hurry to the full swing of its hinges. A man looked out and seeing my brothers' father struggling with my weight and the force of the wind, jumped down to take me and shoved me up into the cab. I crawled onto the bed in the back of the cab and watched as the adults climbed in and exchanged names and storm stories. Before they could finish making plans of how to get to safety before the fuel in the truck ran out, we were thrown forward from the force of a jolt to the back of the 18 wheeler. The men went out to investigate, holding onto the sides of the truck for guidance. They returned with a shocked woman, whom they had helped from her car after it had run into the nearly invisible white truck. My mother took her onto the bed, wrapped her in blankets and held her till she stopped shaking.

A white truck with a huge plough on the front stopped beside the cab and honked it's horn. Windows were rolled down and a shouted conversation ensued. He was from the farm just up the road and had been making short forays into the storm to gather stranded travellers. We followed his flashing hazard lights until we reached his home. Once inside we were greeted by the sight of 12 others all sheltering in the warmth of his hospitality. His wife had hot drinks and stew for us and the 8 more that arrived before the end of the storm. I fell asleep with my head nestled in the warmth of the smelly farm dogs' fur, on the rag rug in front of the fire. The voices swirled around me, gently eddying and murmuring in a syncopated rhythm to the storm wailing outside.

After our car was dug out and the engine block thawed, we managed to get to the hospital to bring my brother home the next day. He looked at me, in my coat with my arms open wide and burst into tears. Rejected and dejected, I began to cry too. Our mom sighed as she gathered us both into her arms.

Skipping skunk kittens

I woke with a tickly feeling in the pit of my tummy. It was Easter and my mommy had said that there might be a surprise waiting for me in the kitchen today. I slipped out from under my covers, wincing as my bare feet made contact with the air. It was still very cold this time of the year in Eastern Canada and the old wooden house didn't have much in the way of insulation.

I got my dressing gown and slippers on and crept downstairs without waking anybody. I hated to share my surprises even if just by having someone observe my experience of it. I was a strange child and at 9 years old, fully conscious of my odd ways but unwilling to change them to suit others. My mother encouraged this and most other signs of my independence. Differences were expected to be celebrated in our peaceful lives and the love began at home!

I glimpsed a scrap of paper glowing on the wood of the table, illuminated by the bright but still cold sunshine. A spray of rainbows littered the table, spun by the prism which was suspended by a length of fishing line tacked into the window frame. I walked over to the table, avoiding the floor boards which I knew would creak the loudest and read the note.

Turn to face the kitchen cupboards and walk 10 steps forward

A clue taped onto on one of the cupboards displayed the words open me in purple crayon and inside was a figurine of a bunny covered in felt flocking with wide open eyes and stiff little whiskers, ooooh I just loved him! I kept him for years moving him from one house to the next in our many moves around the country. Under the bunny was another scrap of paper. This one was decorated with drawings of brightly coloured jelly beans, fluffy yellow chicks and the following words in green crayon:

Walk 6 big steps and turn right then walk 5 extra big steps.

I ended up in front of the bookcase looking at the word BATHROOM spelt out in brightly coloured jelly beans with a bowl beside the word piled high with more of the same. I ate a large handful straight away, stuffing my mouth full so that when I chewed there were jelly beans everywhere in my mouth; on top of my tongue and in the spaces between my gums and cheeks. I had not yet learned the lingering fear that comes from an episode of choking.

Peeking into the bathroom, feeling suddenly shy for no discernible reason, perhaps overwhelmed by the unusual excess of sweet treats; I spied a fluffy yellow chick perched on a soft blue blanket. I tucked the chick under my arm and draped the blanket over my head. Hidden, I then popped my thumb in and sucked away for a while rubbing the sating edges of the blanket across my upper lip.

Eventually I heard my mother's voice float through the ceiling.

'Please take the stuff out of the dryer for me honey.'

'Okaaaay! The Easter bunny left me stuff mommy and notes telling me where to find it! How does he hold a pen?'

'Magic curly girl, magic!' came my mom's drowsy reply buoyed by a hint of laughter.

I opened the dryer door, reached in while looking behind me to grab the basket and knocked something over inside which made a loud clunk! Inside the dyer was a very large, solid chocolate Easter bunny with a basket full of speckled candy eggs on his back! He had a white ribbon dotted with coloured spots tied around his neck which had a note tucked inside it.

Please share your presents with your sweet little brother, love from the Easter Bunny xo

Later on that day my mom, brother and I went for a walk. My brother's father had been given his marching orders by this time and we no longer had to share our mother's affections. I thought this quite wonderful but I expect my brother at almost a year of age was not even aware of his father's existence let alone his banishment. Mom stopped suddenly, crouched down, took my hand and pointed it with hers.

'Look!'

My brother and I looked and saw a mommy skunk with her 3 little kittens out for a walk. Except that baby skunk kittens didn't walk, they bounced with their little tails held straight up in the air, just like the cartoon skunk Peppy Le Phew. I was overwhelmed by their exuberance, touched by their sheer joy for life. The tears welled in my eyes until they brimmed and ran down my cheeks. My mom stroked the tears off my cheeks, her eyes glistening too, locked in the moment with me

Ghosties come a 'leanin

We were at my dad's for a visit! I was so excited. I had no recollection of this man yet I loved him with an almost palpable force. I realise now how much that must have pissed my mother off. Here was her daughter, besotted with a man who had no contact with her or paid any child maintenance since they'd separated when I was 18 months old. Perhaps even worse, there I was fawning around him like an eager puppy. I am willing to bet she wore her teeth down by grinding them out of sheer frustration. I clung to my dad, scared to let him out of my sight, convinced he would vanish once again. I think that more than wanting to see me again; he desired reconciliation with mom. As far as I know my mother had absolutely no desire to rekindle that old flame, though it is entirely possible that she had hedged her bets and neglected to mention this fact to my dad at this point.

He lived on the other end of Canada, on the West Coast or 'Lotus Land' as he often called the little Island he lived on. He'd paid for our airfare and it was mine and my brother's first trip on a plane. My brother had a 'sookey' blanket and without it would never settle. Mom kept making nervous jokes about how our life would be a misery if we didn't have his 'sookey' and guess what we forgot? Why or how I don't remember but that plane flight was sheer hell for him, us and all the other passengers who had to put up with his wailing for the majority of the trip. He was bereft, in a strange environment, refusing to be comforted by the nearness of our presence. That was a shock to me and I wailed to mom, 'why doesn't he like us anymore?' She, of course, had no answer to a question that she may have felt like wailing herself!

I don't know how my mom kept so calm, why she didn't burst into tears herself. She must have been in turmoil, wondering what she was going to have to deal with when she came face to face with my father again after all those years. I felt sorry for my baby brother and desperately wanted him to settle down but nothing would soothe him.

Eventually he cried himself to a fretful, restless unconsciousness. The silence was blessed, you could almost sense the whole atmosphere in the plane relax simultaneously. After a short while during which we all enjoyed my brother's silence, we began our descent and through the window I saw some pretty strange stuff. Green, there was green everywhere, trees, grass, it was amazing! The whole land was green, turning to grey or blue where it met bodies of water or the occasional snow capped mountain.

We had left a city full of snow and ice, our plane climbing up into even whiter cloud banks and emerging from them a few hours later into a lush, vibrantly green land. At that point I was a bit nervous about meeting my dad for the 'first' time and avoided eye contact with him, using the mesmerising beauty of the landscape as an excuse. As I grow older, my absences from the Island where I grew up become more prolonged, but I still feel this way whenever I first glimpse that lush green land with the Spanish moss growing from the trees in the vast forests.

At some point during this holiday I had felt very sick one evening and mom had put me in the bath. I can count on one hand the amount of times I have vomited in my life but each time since then, I have put myself into a bath and each time, just like the first time, it hasn't worked! So why do I find a bath so comforting when I am unwell? Perhaps the memory of my mother's tenderness, perhaps the nearness of the toilet...

After I had been sick, my mom got me out, helped dry my shaky body off and then after saying good night to her and my dad, I went to bed. Exhausted I fell asleep quickly, lulled by the sound of my brothers deep breathing floating across the room from his crib. Some time later I woke to see two white shapes in the room. A mannish shape leaning over me and a womanish shape leaning over my brother. I smiled and mumbled goodnight to them both thinking they were mom and dad checking on us before they went to bed. They left without saying anything and they next morning I asked them why. They both said they had not been into our room at all that night and that it must have been visiting ghosties. My mom has a few wild tales to tell of ghosts in the farmhouse where she grew up and firmly believes such things exist. I find the very thought makes me squirm! These are the only ghosts that I have ever seen and they were soft and gentle in their behaviour. So why am I terrified of the supernatural now?

Fog enchantment

I closed the front door to my dad's house softly so as not to wake the sleeping household. Leaning on the waist high edge of the covered porch, I looked out at the ocean. Dark grey water embraced the white clouds at the horizons margin. The heavy atmosphere drew the briny scent of the driftwood and seaweed laden beach towards the shore, infiltrating my untainted senses. The tiny hairs on my face bristled as the salty mist settled on them. Gentle waves rustled and murmured, crooning to the pebbles on the beach; leaving behind tendrils of foam that fizzed around them before sinking into the sand.

Following my urge to be closer to this syncopation, I crossed the wide path that lead to the narrow beach. I stepped down from the path to the beach, making my way around the driftwood which rested on the rocks till I reached the damp pebbles which led to the water's edge. As I crunched across them, crabs scuttled sideways, snapping their claws at me in aggressive mock challenges before vanishing under the nearest shadow.

A seagull reeled and swept into the water. Paddling up to the water's edge, it clumsily approached me on dry land, tilting its head endearingly to see if I might have a treat to share. I threw a crab which was snapped up hastily, an enigmatic look emerging around the sea gull's eyes as it swallowed. Suddenly, it took flight, vanishing in moments as the fog wrapped around the white and grey blend of its feathers.

I looked around, astonished to see that I too was surrounded by the fog and only able to see the water's edge at the peripheries of the cotton wool wrapped world. Sitting on a large bit of driftwood, I found some seaweed and began to squeeze the dried husks. The air escaped with an addictive muted pop. Periodically I looked up at my dream like surroundings; eyelids lulled half closed by the peacefulness of it all. I stayed on the beach for a long time, ignoring the creeping dampness which had begun to sink into my bones.

Eventually my mother's voice lured back into my other world, the one which was redolent with the smells of fresh baked bread, coffee and the sound of my brother's delighted giggles at my sudden appearance in the room. I kissed his silky skin and he blessed me with a splat of his hand, wet from being chewed on by his budding gums. Dad's beard bristled against my cheek and mom smelled of roses, brewers yeast and mint. I don't know why, she just did back then and still does to this day.

My curls hung damply against my neck and cheeks and I caught a drip of salty water as it plipped off the end of my nose. Holding it up on the tip of my finger it seemed to glow as it reflected the dining room light. Overwhelmed by my experiences in the soft fog that morning, I said not a word. My mother, intuitive to my moods and who believed children should be given roots and wings, let me cling to my other world till I was able to let it go.

My world takes a sideways step

After Christmas that year, the world as I knew it ground to a halt and then took a giant step sideways. Mom had made a decision which would grow in significance as the years passed. We were to stay on the West Coast, permanently! Not with my father as I had hoped but we would live on the same Island. I was ecstatic, grateful for at least this partial realisation of my dream.

To be able to live forevermore in this lush green land where I could go out to play in the middle of winter wearing simply a rain coat and some rubber boots was akin to living a dream. On this small Island the beach and forest were both within easy reach. For a child as inquisitive as I, to be able to explore at will was marvellous; we had no television and my overactive brain needed constant stimulation.

I have no recollection of being aware of the need to be wary of strangers. It was a simpler time then, before the news programmes began to really focus on highlighting every country's despicable events under one umbrella of televised daily devastation. I knew that the move to this milder climate meant the days of struggling into an all in one snow suit would be gone. This process often left me worn out before I'd had a chance to struggle through knee high snow to a clear spot where I could fall back and then move my arms and legs outwards and in until I'd made a fairy shape in the snow. There wasn't a lot else a small child could do in deep snow and the long winters meant I spent a lot of time bouncing off the walls with boredom much as any other caged creature does.

There was of course a new man in her life. There were always men around vying for my mother's affections, drawn to her like ants to sweet. Like a neglected child, or an addict (and I am convinced that one variety or another, often emerges from the ashes of the other), she would indulge herself in the delights they dangled before her. These were times of sexual awakening for women of her generation and with the advances in contraception, there was no reason for her to even consider not succumbing to erotic temptations. I of course, resented each and every one of these men, all except my father, in whom she appeared to have no sexual interest anyways. I hated the fact that anyone besides my brother and I could cause her eyes to light up in that way, unaware that these men provided her with a release we never could.

I was to start school at the local elementary that January. My mother was going back to the East Coast to pack up and arrange for shipment of our belongings. My breast feeding brother would travel with her but if I was to do so I would be late starting school. I remember being offered the choice of whether to remain behind so that I could start school on time or travel with my mother.

I knew that I would have to stay with the man who was my mother's latest playmate as staying with my dad was not an option, though I can not remember why. Perhaps he had already begun fishing for extra cash as the herring season started early each new year. Perhaps he was not ready to take on the care of a young child, not even one whom he referred to as his 'love child'. I don't know and I have never wanted to know badly enough to ask either of them. As we had only arrived at some point in December, I had not yet had a chance to make any friends. The thought of starting school as the 'new girl' was bad enough without starting after everyone else and so I opted to stay behind in 'Lotus Land'.

Too independent for my own good

So there I was, a 9 1/2 year old, spending the week on my own with a stranger. A man who had in a short space of time managed to convince my mother that he was capable of caring for her girl. I am certain I too played my part in creating this situation for myself by convincingly insisting that I wished to stay. I was used to getting my own way and knew how to argue my case effectively with my mom. Time would prove this skill to not always be in my best interest.

The reason I wished to stay behind was two-fold. Partly to relieve the burden (as I perceived it) of her having to travel with two children all that distance, pack up and arrange for shipment of our belongings and then travel back, all in one week. Partly for the reasons mentioned previously, I wanted to begin the school term with the rest of my class as I assumed that was all it would take for me to fit in easily.

I may have been a bit of a wild child but I was also extremely perceptive. I could clearly see that the move would be a lot to organise and even more so with two children demanding her attention. Even at that age I was too independent for my own good! It took me another 2 1/2 decades to learn that being dependant upon someone was actually quite a pleasant sensation.

Little did I know that I would not be accepted by the majority of my classmates no matter how hard I tried to fit in. Although English was my first language, French had been the language of my education and that of my school friends in Eastern Canada. So I had no idea of how to mix with my peers in an English speaking school. I didn't understand the rules of these new playground games and stood on the sidelines pretending that I didn't care that I hadn't been chosen for either team. Pretending that I preferred to have the time to learn the rules.

I don't remember much about the week my mom and brother were away except that I ate at least one meal in front of a black and white telly. I am not sure why it was there (and it certainly didn't stay there for long), but I was thrilled to be able to watch it as I had never lived in a house with a telly before. I can't remember what I watched but am sure I would have been riveted by any programme just for the experience. I got some pretty strange looks when I went to school and gushed excitedly about my telly watching experience. TVs were not a new experience for my classmates and this served to further highlight my differences, another mark in the wrong place on my school 'cool' card.

In sharp contrast to the harshness of the school playground was the amazing Island we lived on. It was covered in ancient forests with moss hanging from the tree branches. There was, as far as I could tell from my short time here, miles of beaches. The shores lined with rocks more than sand which was marvellous for a young child who wanted to explore the marine life left in shallow pools when the tide went out. I loved to lose myself in the sounds, colours and tactile experiences it had to offer. As I would continue to discover, it was filled with remote, serene places that soothed my soul.

Today the Island is home to many millionaires (which somehow put a slight tarnish on my minds' image of it), however the resident population remains at no more than 4000. Back in the 70's it could not have been more than 1000.

Although there were a few popular tourist resorts for fishing and sightseeing, as well as an Indian reserve, and a rather large group of Christian families living on a huge property which bordered a lake; the majority of the resident population were hippies eking out a living in rural proprieties with no electricity or running water. As an adult I long to move back there, to buy the house I have long coveted on the hill that borders the shores of a secluded bay. To be able to drift in the silence and solitude of that wonderful Island that, in places, is a land that progress, thankfully, forgot.

School becomes a struggle

My mother and brother returned with a few suitcases, the rest of our belongings were being shipped to us. She got a job almost straight away working in the post office and also doing the books for the grocery store. The two businesses were owned by the same couple. I thought they frowned too much.

I began to sleep badly, dragging myself to school each morning, experiencing surges of rage as soon as I stepped foot onto the school grounds. Flames of anger would flicker as they grew, feeding on the sheer volume of their playground antics. All of which I was excluded from.

Lonely and increasingly socially awkward, I withdrew into myself. The noise and organised chaos of the school playground was becoming overwhelming. Each morning I would stomp along the concrete path, head down past the chattering, jesting, groups of my peers; their shrieks of laughter vibrating in my head as I walked quickly towards the front doors of the school. Blessed silence smoothed my jangled nerves as they closed behind me and I would sit in the soft quiet of the library until class began.

'Stupid and loud!' I would rant to myself, 'Why do they need to talk so loudly?' Their voices would shout snatches of conversation at friends nearest them, to other children scattered around the school yard, in fact at anyone besides myself.

I sought adult attention more than ever as teachers always responded when I spoke to them. I thought they liked me and was blissfully unaware that they were more than likely just being polite. I now cringe when I look back on these times from an adult's perspective. Did they find me annoying? Did they pity me? Did they discuss behavioural adaptation techniques in relation to my isolation and blatant non conformity?

I discovered that all the basic subjects were slightly off kilter when taught in English instead of French and began to struggle, especially with math. By that spring I had gone from being a first class student to a 'struggling at the bottom of the class' one. Now not only was I a complete loser with no friends and hippie parents but I was also the class dunce. The children in my year at school took to calling me 'Decay' which was a play on the first letters of my fore and surname; Denyse Kirkby.

Something glorious happened at the end of that awful, ego crushing school semester though; I made a friend! Kathy started school a month or so before the summer break. Kim was her twin sister. Kim was instantly a hit with the popular kids, in the way that some people are. Kathy was not. She had a birth defect in the form of a flat crinkled nose with no cartilage in it. I do not know if she gravitated towards me because no one else offered friendship or if she would have liked me anyways.

I didn't question her motives. My stomach flipped with the excitement of having a friend of my own. We spent class breaks sitting with our backs against the school wall, talking, giggling and pretending we didn't care that no one else would play with us. I walked to school each morning with lightness in my heart, timing my arrival to coincide with Kathy's.

By the last days of school before the summer break, the other kids had spotted that we were becoming firm friends and they turned on us like a pack of wolves stalking a couple of cornered deer. They began calling her 'Flea-bag'. We endured the bullying with grim determination because we thought we had no other option. We knew that a summer of freedom from school would begin in just a few days.

Mapping

I think I need to try and draw a figurative map of the property we lived on. If you stood facing the house the garden was behind and to the right, the garage at one far end with the driveway going past this. A beautiful Alder tree was behind and to the left bordering the other side of the driveway and in front of the beginning of the blackberry brambles that stretch the length of the drive.

The house was cedar sided and cedar shingles covered the roof. That house was a fire trap. A fire trap still waiting to occur as far as I am aware; now that is what I call luck. In time the attic was converted into an artist's studio for Dick and a small part of it made into a bedroom for me. A gorgeous conservatory with stained glass at the bottom and steps made from huge slabs of stone leading up to it soon became a feature to the front of the house.

To the near left of the house was our lawn which stopped abruptly as it butted up against the edge of the woods. Inside that bit of woods was a huge uprooted tree in which I would make a fort to play in, but that is a post for another time.

The woods came within 500 feet of our house at the back. Except for two trees with very wide trunks, this area close to the house was sparsely treed. It was full of wonderful smells and sights like toadstools, Spanish moss hanging from the tree branches, sound absorbing carpets of pine needles and fungi growing from the tree bark.

To the right of the house, just past the wood shed, was a grassy area which sloped upwards and at the top edge was an abandoned wooden structure which must have been someone's' house at one time. One day while playing on it, my left leg slipped into a hole between 2 boards. One knee and my hip bent causing my groin and top of my right leg to slam against the floor board with my left dangling down through the hole. I had badly strained my ligaments and limped for weeks! The structure was soon torn down and in its place the (previously hidden) old well was used to feed a stream on which our ducks could waddle down to paddle around on a large pond near the garden.

In between this structure and the wood shed was the area which would become home to our chicken coop, currently it was home to a nice crop of marijuana plants. The stems were as thick as my wrists and I had to tilt my head right back to see the dark green tops of the plants. They seemed impossibly tall, taller than Dick. He had to use a ladder to get high enough to cover them with green tarpaulin sheeting each time the police helicopter circled the Island. I thought this terribly exciting, having no idea of exactly how illegal growing pot was.

The police set up their headquarters on the property that bordered ours in the next year. We were separated by a 12 foot ditch and nothing more, which obviously put an end to the 'grow your own dope' experiment. The rapidly cleared patch of ground was put to good use as a chicken run. The local raccoons found them irresistibly tempting but that story as well as all of the others I've remembered while writing this will be told some other point.

De-rocking and fencing the garden

School was over for the summer and instantly all the playground nastiness was compartmentalised and locked safely away as I looked forward to the relief of days of fun in the sun. Children's psyches are remarkably resilient, which is lucky as mine would have a varied range of insults to process and overcome during the next 5 years.

I fell in love that summer...with an Alder tree! It was the tallest tree on the property and I loved to sit on one of the branches. It was higher than the house and the height gave me a sense of power. The branches were evenly spaced round the trunk and easy to climb, once I had figured out how to swing myself up onto the lowest branch. I would sit quietly, watching the view with my cheek pressed onto the smooth warm bark.

Even with the tree in full leaf I could see most everything I wanted to from my green shaded perch. With my back to the ditch that ran along the far side of the long driveway, I could look ahead and see the house or to my right and see the large vegetable garden. Dick said we were going to build a fence to keep the deer out. Dick was the man my mom had fallen in love with, the man who owned this property. He had a lot of plans for this summer and it seemed that I would be expected to work along side him to help each project reach fruition. I didn't mind at first; it all sounded very exciting during the planning and discussion stage.

The fence was to be 6 feet high and made of wire strung from cedar wood. It had to be that high to keep the deer out. As lovely as they were to see, grazing on the 3/4 of acre we lived on, they were an absolute menace to anything like a cultivated garden. Dick dug holes for the fence posts and then pounded them in deep with a sledge hammer.

At regular intervals I would hear him shout 'Stop wasting time and get over here to see what real work is all about!'

He expected me to steady the fence wire as he fastened it onto the each post. Quite a challenge when the wire was almost double my height and meant I had to stand with my hands over my head, not daring to move till he was finished, praying he would hurry as I felt the blood drain from my arms.

At just 10 years of age, I had earned a well deserved reputation for clumsiness and an unerring ability to maim myself so I was kept well away from the sharp tools and instead sent to work doing what he referred to as 'wasting time'. By this he meant de-rocking the garden soil. There were hundreds and thousands of them! They were all shapes and sizes and many were just below the surface and easily got at.

I would rake over the soil, gather up a handful and transfer them to a waiting bucket. This bucket when full would get transferred to a waiting wheelbarrow. Each full-ish wheelbarrow got emptied on a rockery in progress. The rockery began just to the left of the garden, just past the garage. It bordered a moderate length of the 12 foot ditch that ran along the outer edge of the property, following the line of the drive-way down to the road hundreds of metres away.

You wouldn't be wrong in thinking the de-rocking process sounded like a one child assembly line. Dick had no issues with child labour. In the tradition of the Medieval English he seemed to firmly believe that was one of the reasons for having children. His two sons, one younger and one older than I, lived in England with their mother so it was left to me to pick up the slack. My brother, only just walking, was left to totter around nearby, within earshot. I chattered away to him, desperate for the day when he would begin talking, blissfully unaware that once he started he wouldn't stop!

Mom worked mornings in the post office and each day dragged until she came home. I was physically exhausted and emotionally numb without her presence nearby. Even though the sun shone, there was no brightness when I was on my own with Dick. I soon learned to keep quiet and to be happy to be able to work out of his reach; edging out of his sight whenever possible to sit and drift away on clouds of thought.

Once mom came home and joined us for the afternoon session, the world seemed to speed up and sparkle again. She was so happy toiling on the land, putting her personal imprint on the place she had chosen to call home. I have never had what might be termed a 'silly bone' but her enthusiasm and silliness were infectious. Shaking her head in mock disgust, she would look at my brother and me in the garden. My face set with a sullen look of determination and him toddling round, slowly transferring half the garden soil onto his!

'Oooh you are such a grubby boy! I think we'll pop you in the washing machine once we've finished here. What do you think Denyse, will our old wringer washer be up to the job or should we take him to the Laundromat and use their super duper whizzy ones?' Eventually my laughter

would join hers, ringing out and bouncing off the forest trees
that edged the property.

French kissing

That summer in the year I turned 10 is marked in my memory as the first time Dick ever made an overtly sexual advance on me. Well the first one I remember, they may have been ones before this that I didn't register for what they were intended. One evening, I went to give him and mom my usual good night kiss on the cheek. He suddenly turned his face so his lips were on mine and then shoved his tongue into my mouth. Knowing I should tone down my reaction to prevent offending him, but unable to contain my revulsion I leapt back from his mouth and shouted,

'Urgh Gross!'

'You were a frog before you moved here, that is how French people kiss, and it is called a French kiss!' Dick's face was blandly innocent, eyes wide with feigned surprise.

Mom, whose attention had been distracted by something, turned to me in surprise. 'What?'

'He shoved his tongue in my mouth!' I lifted my pyjama top and scrubbed his saliva off my lips.

'Dick, I don't think she needs to know that kind of thing yet', mom admonished him with a mock disapproving tone. She too was learning to modulate her words to prevent his temper flaring out of control.

I can imagine her thought processes: She could see that I was okay; nothing terrible had happened had it? She had been in the room all the time. Simply a misunderstanding which luckily had not escalated into one of Dick's verbal rants about how spoiled and melodramatic I was.

I went to bed, feeling ashamed of causing a fuss, disgust still coiled in my belly.

Swinging

If I sat in my alder tree and looked just past the branch on which my tire swing was hung, I could see into the woods that stretched from the road to the lawn. In those woods was my secret fort. It was made from the nooks, tangles and crannies found in an up rooted tree. Within reaching distance, if I stretched arms length out from the top of the snarled roots, was a Fir tree. This is where I had tied the opposite end of the rope that my pet cat was tethered to.

When I had been told that I couldn't keep the starving cat that was hanging around the house, I snuck it and some food to my fort. I thrilled with the excitement of having this secret that loved only me and purred with desperate, needy, delight. In my 9-year-old naivety, it never occurred to me that the cat might get caught up whilst jumping down from the root snarl. After finding the cat strangled; air currents making it twist gently on the noose formed by the tether, I never returned to the fort except in my mind, where to this day, I frequently make the trip to apologise again and again to that poor cat.

Please don't feed me I am already stuffed

'What will we do if there is no money coming in Dick?'

The anxiety in my mom's voice woke me as effectively as if I had been doused with a bucket of freezing water.

'It isn't going to hurt us to go without a meal or two, all we need to worry about is keeping up with the payments on the property. Easily covered by your earnings at the post office!' His chair feet clunked onto the wooden floor as he shifted his weight forward.

They were arguing in the kitchen on the other side of the thin walls of the room I shared with my brother.

'But what about the kids? They can't be expected to go without if you've got a lull between jobs!' Worry broke her voice on the end of the sentence.

'For fucks sake woman! This is real life not some charity for your brats! You spawned them you feed them. I've got a chance to start up a landscaping business and all you can do is throw barriers in my way'. After all I've done for you, his low and menacing tone implied.

I climbed down from my bunk and into my brother's, wrapping my arms round his silky warmth. Pretending I was protecting him from the harshness but in reality doing little more than comforting myself as he was fast asleep. I too fell asleep, my traumatised ears soothed by the predictable waves of his breathing.

My mom began to sew stuffed animals, made of scraps of fabric, bit of jeans, old flannel nighties, ripped pillow cases, anything she could find in the thrift stores bargain bin. The first one she made for my brother and inspired by his delight, she made more and sold them at craft fairs, and through notices on community boards. She still has a picture of my brother asleep in his crib, diapered bum in the air, with that bear beside him.

Several years later, my brother lined up all his handmade animals in a makeshift zoo and propped up a sign which read, 'Please don't feed me, I am already stuffed'. When my son was born she made him a giant mouse. We love his floppy, stripey ears; that eccentric signature which is definitive of my mother's character.

She was too proud to take the easy way out and collect welfare cash handouts and so was no stranger to hard work. When we lived in Eastern Canada she had worked at the library and also had taken on part time work for a maple syrup farm. Our small living room was filled with cans. She was paid to put all the labels on empty cans and in early spring we would go there and help fill all cans and bottles with the maple syrup. I wrote about this great place in Chapter 9 - The Candy Tree Forest. They paid well and paid in cash which meant she didn't have to claim the earnings.

Around this time we also acquired a cat, or rather I should say, he acquired us. One day he appeared, strolling casually out of the woods behind the house and promptly made us his own. I adored him but my mother was the clear winner in the challenge to win his affections. He would rub his smelly head on her, huge purrs rumbling as she chattered to him about nothing in particular.

Mom said he had probably been a human in a past life. She was always coming out with statements like this in a tone of voice that made it clear she'd suffer no disagreement on the subject but for once I agreed with her completely. That very first day, Kitty, as we imaginatively called him, caught two mice in the kitchen! He was obviously a wise cat and knew that he had to quickly demonstrate to Dick that he could pay his own way

Cannabis raids

We were hard at work picking Blackberries on late summer day. Mom and Dick were at the height of picking frenzy, a state I now find myself in at the same time of year; trying to get one last harvest of berries before the season ends. This session was to gather enough fruit to make wine. They each had huge pails and I had a large shallow basket suspended from my neck with cord. This left my hands free to pick and prevented any moaning about how sore my arms were from having to hold the rapidly increasing weight of the berry container.

I was hot, scratched to bits from the brambles, my fingers stained purple from the warm juice that tasted of perfumed sunshine. I had eaten my fill, bored stupid by the endless repetition of the task; reach, get scratched, grasp fruit, pluck it, get scratched, pull away, brush against stinging nettle, drop berry into basket. I was contemplating how to convince them of my desire, indeed my sheer desperation to stop picking and go do something else, when we heard the Police helicopter.

Out of habit Dick tensed, ready to run to his 'grow your own dope' experiment and camouflage the plants with a couple of sheets of green tarpaulin. Remembering that he had cut down and stripped all his stalks of their cannabis leaves, buds and seed, he relaxed and tilted his head skywards. Mom and I copied him, shadowing our eyes from the glare of the sun which bounced off the landing skids. The thunderously loud machine circled over Dick's property and headed towards the school. I watched in amazement as the helicopter began to descend.

I looked beseechingly at my mom she nodded, 'Go on then but don't get in their way!'

I raced down the rest of the gravel driveway, crossed the road using only my ears to tell me if there was any traffic heading towards me. My eyes were intent on one thing only, the sight of the helicopter bouncing gently to a stop on the school field! I emerged from behind Mrs Hayward's house, whose property bordered the school, just in time to see two policemen hop out with their heads tilted down. I looked to see what was so fascinating on the ground but it just looked like the school field to me except the grass was being blown flat against the ground! Perhaps they'd never seen such green grass before I thought and I was just about to shout 'That grass sure is green, eh?'

Luckily my mouth snapped shut on the words as the police men ran a few feet away from the machine and then stood upright facing the helicopter. Once the blades had come to a halt, they walked back, opened a door and began to pull out enormous amounts of cannabis plants. I watched silently as they piled all the plants on a patch of concrete which began where the playing fields ended. They put on face masks before one of them stepped forward and lit the leafy mass. Billows of grey smoke rose from the raided plants. I wondered if the men were getting stoned despite the masks and if they were enjoying it. I was blissfully unaware that I would start a grass fire of my own the following year, on the very property I stood on to watch the police this day.

By train, boat and car

My aunt who had lived with us in Eastern Canada soon joined us on the Island. Along with her came my cousins, Bobbie and her younger sister Joanne. Mom and Auntie Carol had rarely lived far from each other for any period of time. It was inevitable that their familial gravity would draw them into each other's orbit once again.

She was escaping a destructive relationship and we were welcoming her into an equally dysfunctional space.

My aunt and cousins had travelled by train for many days to reach Vancouver. Mom had given her the money to pay for her and my cousins' tickets and now mom, my brother and I were on our way to collect them from the station. This was an 8 hour trip by car and ferry for us; mere increments in comparison to the arduous, days long train journey they had just experienced.

When mom told him she was giving the money to auntie Carol so she could escape to the Island, he stamped round the house glowering and muttering about his hard earned cash being used as a charity fund. How quickly he had forgotten that it was, in part, due to the sales of mom's stuffed animals that their bank account was so well padded, even more so now that the mortgage on the property was paid off! However, by the day of their arrival he had cheered up. I assume he was entertaining himself with all sorts of fantasies about coming to the rescue of yet another young woman with young children. What a hero...I am not sure where he found the strength to carry around that ego!

Auntie Carol and my cousins moved into a trailer home just down the end of the road, just a short walk in return for a lot of comfort. I was always a strange child but was rapidly becoming prickly and shut down. At her home I didn't have any figurative pillars to perch on, precariously balanced by the conflicting weights of Dick's unrealistic expectations. I was allowed to just 'be me' and when my mother and aunt were cosied together in her little trailer; they revelled in my uniqueness and nurtured my individuality. A healing balm indeed. I made sure to protect my fragile inner self by wrapping it in emotional cotton wool, surrounded by a solid brick block before we left to go 'home' each time. It was my gift from my mom and aunt and Dick wasn't getting a piece of it!

My aunt had an air of aloofness and mystique which was in fact an extreme case of shyness. She began to attract male attention and soon began to date and heal under their tender ministrations to her ego. Dick's business partner, Gary, had a single brother. My aunt began to date him a couple of years after her arrival on the Island soon fell pregnant and they began to live together.

By the time this happened I had already run away to my aunt's cramped trailer on one occasion! This would prove to be much more difficult once she moved in with Uncle Doug. The new house was farther up the road and would soon include my newest (and loudest) cousin, Gregie. My first and most frequent memories of Gregie are that he cried constantly. More than 20 years after his arrival, my mom and I would slump onto the couch, linked in exhaustion, listening to my son TJ's echoingly familiar unrelenting crying and experience a simultaneous shiver of deja vu!

Menarche

The year I turned 11, I began to have menstrual periods. I can remember quite clearly the first time I bled as I am sure so many other women can. I was at someone's house, began to have stomach pains and expecting to be overcome with diarrhoea, I decided I had better head home. When I got there I went straight to the toilet and found my underpants covered in brown goo.

Mom and Dick's reactions were totally different as you might imagine.

When I called mom into the bathroom to show her the mess in my underpants she said 'Oh my curly girlie, today you have taken your first step to becoming a woman!'. She was so pleased for me that I began to feel proud instead of scared. Mom showed me how to pin a pad on, how a hot water bottle and cups of Yarrow tea would ease my cramps and explained that I must keep track of my periods on a calendar. Then she took me out into the woods in the back of our house to gather pine cones, explaining that these were symbols of fertility, a symbol of the great honour that would be bestowed upon me when I fully became a grown woman. Now that I have the privilege of raining my own child, I realise that she was right; being a mother is truly a great honour. I adored this time we spent together, my brother tagging along but not listening to our conversation. Mom and he looked so beautiful, their faces dappled by the filtered sunlight which drifted down through the pine needled boughs. The moss hanging from the branches glowed as if light from within. I felt special, unique, magical and completely linked to a greater consciousness.

When mom excitedly told Dick the news of my menarche at supper time, his face fell. Leaning towards me, face still and lips stretched against his teeth, he said 'This means you can get pregnant now, so you'd better be careful or you'll end up having a baby and don't be thinking I'll support you and your brat!'

Stunned by his words I looked to mom for guidance; quickly realising she'd be no help for she looked as puzzled as I felt. I knew a man had to put his penis inside a woman's vagina to make a baby. I didn't do that kind of stuff so what was he talking about? He had told us that he had two boys who lived in England with their mother so surely he knew how babies were made?

Dick whipped his eyes from mine to lash them across mom's line of vision which was fixed on his face. 'What?' he barked.

Mom's eyes dropped to her food, her throat twitched and she scooped some food into her mouth. From my vantage point I could see her eyes glisten and I looked away fast. Taking my cue from her, I too began to eat once more. My brother sensed the tension as toddlers do, bashed the table with his spoon and laughed at the cat who was lurking near the cupboard which housed the mouse traps. The conversation moved on to less emotive topics, the tension lessened. I didn't understand why Dick always had to spoil everything! I felt ashamed, vilified, instead of empowered by this example of my body's perfect genetic programming.

When I returned to school the bullies had yet another thing to tease me about. Pads were thick uncomfortable bricks in those days and not particularly absorbent either. So not only did it advertise to the world each time I had my period but I occasionally flooded off the sides of my pad , through my clothes, leaving marks on my school chair.

The school nurse would call my mom to come collect me. Mortified beyond belief, I would leave the school to change my clothes, a sweater tied around my hips which boldly announced the fact that I was trying to hide the stains. Mom despaired for me, sensing my shame, although I refused to discuss anything to do with my periods after that dinner conversation on the night of my first one.

Having been bullied too, she was desperate to help me avoid torment at school and so she searched for alternatives to the easily flooded bricks. Tampons were too big for me, keeping me out of school until my period had finished each month was unacceptable, changing my brick more frequently was impossible as it meant leaving class too often to go unnoticed, I hated the idea of dark clothing or the suggestion that I come home each lunch time to change as everyone would notice! Eventually mom found an acceptable alternative, natural sea sponges which were small, soft and quite absorbent, needing to be changed only a few times during the school day.

There was only one catch... when saturated, the sponge had to be rinsed out and obviously I couldn't do it in the girls' toilet. I got permission to use the nurses' toilet but had to sneak into it hoping none of the other kids would see me. I could tell that the school nurse thought it was weird that I was using a sea sponge and I sure as hell didn't want anyone else finding out!

The true intent of the panty paintings

Dick celebrated the completion of the stone steps leading to the conservatory by doing the first in what would become a yearly series of panty painting.

The house was deceptively beautiful, with stone steps leading to the glass fronted porch. Each year I stood on those steps, wearing cut off jean shorts with a peep view of panties covered in tiny blue flowers. My body positioned just so and daring to take only shallow breaths; until he had finished painting and allowed me to change position. No casual observer could detect the extent of the madness inside that house. For even those panty paintings portrayed an air of innocence

One day, when I had come in from school, a pair of my panties had been pinned to the door. No, not on the outside door, the madness was more calculating than that! The panties were pinned to my bedroom door. Sketched on the white cotton fabric was a pair of labia, a urethra, a clitoris and pubic hair. I backed away, hands covering my eyes.

'You uncultured brat!' he raged. 'If you don't want me to leave your filthy panties lying around, then stop walking around dressed like a slut!'

Tight lipped and pale, I looked down at my jeans and t-shirt, in a silent rebuke. I knew the true intent of the painted panties.

A Dream Poem

This is a poem I wrote about a dream I had when I was about 12. Some of the descriptive words 'flake screen of light' and 'motlet' are obviously not 'real' words. They are the words that came to mind as I tried to record exactly what I saw and felt in my dream.

Changing Energies
Sighing
She mixes
Slowly dying
Inside

That flake screen of light
That she made from her motlet
It seemed she would not let
And she screamed with all her might

Enveloping it whole
She gorged herself
Transformed into a mole
Burrowing into a dirt shelf

Settled down
In a new domain
Strangely familiar smells, floating round,
Less pain

Then
The faintest noise
Breath at the front door
Moles head is poised

Face filled with horror

Shuffling down the corridor
Shyly going to investigate
Blind eyes raised to the roar
It's too late

Small and crumpled
Lying on a floor of shame
Seeping blood, fur soft and rumpled
No one's going to take the blame
Now there's no more pain...

Cotton Jenny

Following on from the success of her scrap fabric animals and unbeknownst to me, mom had moved into haute couture on a glorious but miniature scale! One evening after my brother was in bed and Dick had gone out, she unveiled my Barbie doll's new winter wardrobe. It was exquisite! My doll had every piece of clothing imaginable and some I had never even known existed.

Her lingerie was made from twists of lace and wisps of satin, her negligees lined with silk. She had tiny cushions on which to recline of an evening and a crisp linen sheet for her bed. Flowing dresses, extravagant belts and handbags, floaty blouses, jewellery made from tiny buttons, beads and sequins, warm coats, hats and hand muffs; that doll had it all!

This very special gift from my mom allowed me to convince myself that I was quite happy playing on my own. I convinced myself that I couldn't bear to let others touch her delicate clothes and risk them being damaged! I made up elaborate stories about her busy important life where each moment of her time was desired by beautiful people. I would play these fantasies out for hours on end, up in the attic, not noticing the growing dark or dropping temperature until mom would come up and nudge me back into my harsher reality.

It was about this time that my dad moved off the Island and into a rented house in on a larger Island nearby. I used to get to spend a day or two with him on occasional weekends. I loved these escapes from Dick's command. As an adult I can see that it may have been a wrench to let me go even for the day. My dad, who had so far only played a tiny part in my upbringing, would be able to let me temporarily live a different life from the one she imagined to be safe and nurturing for me. I couldn't imagine letting my son go to stay with his birth father. Mind you, this may also be due to the fact that his birth father is not allowed unsupervised contact with him!

The house my dad lived in was shared by his good friend Nghi. They had lived together on the Island and continued to live together for many years more, even after my father remarried...much to my stepmother's understandable disgust! In the over grown back garden was a large cherry tree with branches placed generously for easy climbing into the higher boughs which were fruit laden in the summer. I spent a few happy days ensconced in that tree eating cherries and spitting the seeds onto the ground while watching the birds flit from branch to branch. In the evenings I'd snuggle into the saggy couch cushions and read books or eat the candy that I'd bought with the pennies dad had given me for a treat, while dad and Nghi listened to music, lubricating their auditory pathways with hashish. I'd drift off to sleep listening to Peter, Paul and Mary, John Lennon, Santana, Creedence Clearwater Revival or Gordon Lightfoot.

Dad began to work at Radio shack, running the record player section. I loved to visit him at work because the recessed area where the record players were kept had a sign over it which read 'Len's den'! My dad did look a bit like a grizzly bear with his heavy beard and I thought this was why they had called it that. Looking back from an adult's perspective I am less sure... perhaps it was simply because they were stoned when brainstorming for a name and this was the only one they could come up with. I used to sit in a corner of the dimly lit space and listen to the music, while my dad tried his reclusive best to avoid having to make actual conversation with customers.

Things that go creak in the night

I put Dick's full name into an internet search engine this week, just his name, to see what came up and I got a lot of hits. He is still going strong with the art work I see. Famous on a regional scale nowadays (perhaps even bigger than that) and yes his talent is worthy of that notoriety. I found a bit of art that he had done featuring the house. It is exquisite. I took one glance and my breath was snatched away from me and held captive, lashed tightly against easy escape by the twists of the lines, blinding my eyes with its vivid colours.

I've copied and saved it but don't dare add a copy in this book...I'd hate to be righteously sued by that vile man for breaching copyright. However, If I'd found any of the panty paintings I would have posted them regardless. I feel I've earned that right.

Dick's designed and built his own studio at the top of the house. The studio faced the front of the house. It was brightly light during the day courtesy of two huge windows that ran almost wall to wall. The wooden floor boards reflected any light that touched them and at one end of the studio was a mattress which allowed the studio to double as a spare guest room. I am not sure how Dick could bear to allow anyone near his work in progress. Perhaps he stored it all safely away on those occasions. I know I never set foot anywhere near the studio on my own, not even with the most innocent of intentions; lest the creaking floorboards announce my position and lead to what was always a most unpleasant introduction of flesh to thin bendy branch.

The studio access was through a door in the kitchen, up the stairs and past what became my bedroom that winter. It was a fair sized room under the eaves, to the left of the stairs. I loved the room itself dearly and was allowed to fill it and my double bed with various treasures. Books, live chameleons in a glass tank, a wild mouse in a box which it soon chewed it's way out of, clothes piled carelessly on every surface, my doll and her gorgeous wardrobe, my record player all did their bit to fill my room.

Accorded the honour of sharing my bed were; a bit of rough leather that I rubbed on my upper lip while I sucked my thumb, dried orange peelings, sea shells, more books, clothes which I wanted to warm overnight before putting on in the morning, flowers husks, feathers and a dynamic myriad of other little items. It was a big bed and the space just begged to be filled. I felt safer tucked in amongst all these bed accessories. By day it was a little bit of magic but once dark the spell was broken and I grew to learn to be afraid of creaking stairs and whispers in the night.

The bogeyman is real you see and I have been afraid of things that go 'creak' in the night, to varying degrees, ever since.

Nose candy

'I'm going out. I want this mess cleared and you in bed asleep before I get back.' Dick shoved his chair away from the table.

Eyes down, the sensation of his glare making my scalp crawl, I tilted my forehead towards the table in acquiescence. The house felt lighter somehow, once he'd shut the door...as if all the menace had followed him and fresh air had come to fill the space.

Mom was away for the weekend on a herbalist training course and although she'd left my brother with my aunt, she had decided that I was able to care for myself while Dick was at work. I was torn between pride at my maturity and longing to be ensconced in the cramped but happy environment of the trailer in which my aunt lived.

After I'd washed and put away the dishes, I went to my room. I missed my mom. I missed my brother and wanted to kiss him goodnight before bed like I did every night. I crept downstairs and after listening at the door that separated my stairs to the kitchen to make sure Dick wasn't home yet, I dashed to my brother's room. I intended to grab one of his stuffed animals and fall asleep cuddling something which reminded me of them both.

I lay on his bed, smoothing the toys and lingering over my choice. I must have fallen asleep because I started awake on the end of the sound of the front door closing. My shriek of alarm was masked by the sound of several adult voices. I lay still on my brother's bed, thankful his room was in darkness and away from the social areas of the house such as the joined kitchen and living room areas.

Unfortunately, to get to my bedroom I would need to pass through the kitchen. This was impossible, Dick could not find out I had disobeyed him and so I stayed in my brother's room, weighted by my indecision. I moved from bed to doorway, peering round the corner in the hopes of discovering a suitable moment to get to my room, undetected.

After a long time, the noise levels in the house began to rise, the adults voices and the music contributing to the increasing racket. I noticed a couple slowly making their way towards me, stopping frequently to kiss and touch each other. Trapped between them and the bedroom they were obviously heading towards, I moved behind the door. From this vantage point, with my eyes long since adjusted to the darkness I had a private display of the many ways in which two people can pleasure each other. This fascinated me for a while but I then became annoyed with the sounds of their lovemaking, and began to long for the comfort of my bed.

I moved out the door and pressed myself against the huge wardrobe cloaked in shadows in the corridor. After a bit of manoeuvring, I got myself situated at the right angle to watch the activity in the living room through the reflection in a mirror on the other side of the wall. Most of the adults were slumped on the couches and chairs, talking, fondling each other or swaying with their eyes closed, in rhythm to the music.

A man I didn't recognise rolled up a piece of paper money and handed it to Dick. 'Nose candy?'

Dick snatched it from him with a grin sliding across his mouth, 'Thank you my good man!'

I watched Dick lean over the table, place the straw made of money in his nose and shove this along a white line which disappeared in front of him. Standing up , he ran his finger along the space where the line had been and then rubbed it over his top teeth.

'Money! It's a blast! La, la, la, lah...yeah, yeahhhhhh!' he shouted in tune with the music.

A man next to him opened what looked to me like a white capsule and poured a new white line out. As Dick leaned over this line, I took the opportunity to move in the opposite direction towards the door to the stairs which lead to my room. I lay in bed for what seemed like hours listening to the raucous noise, dreading the mess I'd have to clean tomorrow. I had hoped to go to my aunt's as soon as had Dick left for work.

In the morning, I woke somewhat bleary eyed but desperate to get the house tidy so that I could go see my brother. I knew my mom would be home tonight and although this was some comfort, there was a long Sunday to get through before she arrived. I crept about quietly, trying not to wake Dick and wondering how I could make sure mom found out about the party. Pondering ways to manage to get Dick thrown into a whole world of angst without getting myself into trouble from Dick for tattling on him. As it happened, Dick booked himself a express ticket to the 'doghouse' by being so ill all day that he was still in bed when she arrived home.

My brother and I were snuggled up, contentedly asleep on my aunt's floor as she had refused to send us home while Dick was in such a state. Sometimes the good guys do get to win...

Renaissance fair

A young woman wearing a smock top, her nipples visible through the thin fabric, sat in front of the small stage. Her face was pointed in my direction, looking at me but seeing something else. She weaved her hands in small circles, flipping them backwards and forwards, tilting from the waist, bending side to side, and her hair brushing the grass. The remains of a bemused grin lingered on her generous lips.

The sign above the stage read 'Trippy Tales'. After a long pause during which she gradually ceased the fluid movements of her hands, the young woman returned to the present with a startling movement and launched back into the tale of her last acid trip.

> *The tab melted on my tongue and led me to the valley*
> *so bright*
> *Orange tress pointed me South to a trail as dark as*
> *night*
> *My hands showed me the path*
> *My feet smelled the way*
> *And each time I managed to spiral near the edge*
> *I was drawn back to the core*
> *My blood pulsed, smiling up at me from my skin*
> *As rainbows flashed all around*
> *I sung out my joy*
> *I want more, more, more...*

I stood, then sat and listened as hard as I could, trying to absorb the content of as many conversations as possible at one time. All around I could hear the others gathered around this stage discussing their experiences.

'I was walking through a street in Seattle, when I noticed the houses were pink with green roofs, then the road turned to soup and I was floating on a...' murmured a mans voice.

High pitched, a woman or a boy said 'My sandwich ate my apple!'

A rumbling laugh carried itself to my ears before saying 'The polka dots joined up and I realised that I had been looking at a spaceship...

'I found the universes in the Chantrelle mushrooms!' shrieked someone on the far side of the crowd.

The others turned as one, to look and with that fluid motion, the spell was broken for me and I left to go find my mom. My bare feet sent up puffs of dust from the sun baked soil, the dried grass did little to cushion my bare feet but generously proffered the sweet smell of hay.

The acres of land on which I was currently roaming was host to the Renaissance fair, a yearly event to which thousands came. It was intended as a celebration of all things 'Hippy' and became a rousing success for many years. There were music stages, story sharing stages like the one above, craft stalls, camping areas by the river, the ever popular first aid tent, food vendors, drug and alcohol dealers; all the modern hippy could desire plus a few things they could live without, like the conservative people came to watch the 'freak show'.

I loved every minute we spent there, roaming around the acres filled with stoned happy people. Large groups of children would meet up by the river and skinny dip to cool off. Our parents would drift by, smile and move on to listen to the bands or sleep in the sun. It always seemed to be a sunny day when we were at the fair though I am not sure how much of this is fact and how much is brightened by happy memories. The evenings were warm, camp fires dotted along the river and sweet scented cannabis smoke mingled with the harsher smell of burning wood. The music trickled over on the breeze from the distant stages and conversation was subdued.

My memories of these events are all soothing, gentle and endlessly fascinating! I never forgot the sense of loss I experienced when told the fair was no longer allowed to continue. Noise pollution, waste of farm land, unsavoury goings on...the excuses flowed like mineral stained tap water. Run the tap as long as you like but you'll never quite manage to flush out the unspoken truth. The almost palpable gentleness and goodwill of these gatherings was likely to catch on. However, the prolific drugs of choice were illegal and non-taxable. The hippies who chose to ingest them were wild and extravagant in manner and dress...displaying behaviours which could be classed as different and disturbing to observe if you looked with a jaundiced eye. They spoke willingly with anyone who wished to listen; called each other 'brother' or 'sister' even if it was blatantly obvious they could be of no blood relation! Much better, apparently, to build another bar in order to encourage the consumption of legal drugs like alcohol. They were 'The Establishment'; people who drank to excess and looked much more conservative, with their short hair, sombre dull clothing and shiny red expressionless faces. People who grouped together according to strict criteria which included confusing sub clauses of social class, heritage and ethnicity.

At 12 years old I was already beginning to stereotype the others and these opinions which would remain unchanged to any great extent, for many years. Hippies, on the whole, were 'real' and, with very few exceptions, peaceful; accepting that life flowed with a larger purpose in sight, 'karma counted man', and the conformist others were 'false', sharp edged, cruel people who were inclined to do whatever it took to achieve their goals.

Mothrat

2007 - Chris and I woke simultaneously in the early hours of the morning. We could hear scuttling and scurrying sounds from the vicinity of the floor boards on his side of the bed.

Yikes! Rats? Mice? An infestation of some sort, that was for certain and where were our cats when we needed them? Usually we woke to find one stretched out beside me and the other on top of Chris but this morning there was no sign of them. Chris reminded me that we had a large gap in our floorboards beneath the radiator, oh dear... then he crawled over me and leaped out the bedroom door in search of the cats.

He found them fast asleep on the couch and rudely awakened them, in an attempt to lure them upstairs. His theory was that once there, they would either scare the rodents into staying under the floorboards or to eat them if they dared to surface. We win either way! I could hear him trying to coax them upstairs, but they are not used to friendly tones from us in the middle of the night and kept their distance. I lay listening to the sounds from downstairs and from the floorboards on Chris's side of the bed. The more I concentrated on the scuttling, the more I became convinced it wasn't exactly like the sort of sound I remembered rodents making when I was a child...

1978 - The chicken coop used to get infested with mice; they would burrow tunnels under the coop and carry out raids. I could hear them scuttling about as I cleaned the coop and I often caught a peep of a tiny face watching me boldly as I went about my smelly chore. Their night raids to find any stray chicken feed, would scare the hens that they would go 'off lay'. This loss of eggs plus the terrified clucking coming from the coop at night was enough to send Dick ferret shopping in less than a week. He brought back a white one, it was very hyper, in constant motion, twisting up, down and running around its cage. The smell emanating from it was so strong that it made my eyes water. I thought it looked like a furry snake with ears. We never called it anything but 'the ferret' so I suppose none of us loved it much as a pet. Poor ferret.

It was there to work and work it did, supplementing the meagre rations we gave it with whatever mice it could catch from under the chicken coop. The only food we ever gave it to eat was milk and bread. I used to have to take the dish out and would be frightened when the ferret jumped up at me. I had no idea that it was lonely and hungry, I just thought it wanted to bite me. When Dick wanted the ferret to go after the mice, he would strap it into a leather harness and attach a reel of fishing line to the harness. Away the ferret would scamper, racing through the tunnels, catching and eating his fill. I assume he killed afterwards simply for the fun of as he spent hours under that coop but I never was very fond of that animal so that may be an entirely inaccurate memory. I happen to like ferrets now, although I still think they smell awful and can't quite reconcile the image of a hunter ferret as a cuddly pet. Or the fact that when a ferret nips at me with its sharp teeth, it may actually be giving me a 'love bite'. I much prefer cats; they purr and don't make a habit of biting when I smooth their fur!

The chickens used to get bothered by a much larger predator than the thieving mice. Raccoons were quite fond of our chickens and the ferret was no deterrent, though I am certain he was manic enough to have had a go at chasing raccoons had we let him out. The sound of a raccoon bothering the chickens was quite distinctive from that of the mice scares, much more frantic in pitch. Up we'd leap from our bed and gather at the back door. Once Dick had loaded his 22 rifle, we'd slide into our rubber boots and trail out the door behind him. Why we all went is a mystery. Mom carried the torch and shone it at the raccoon to blind him and frighten him into treeing himself. I trailed along behind them both and kept a firm hold on my brother's hand.

Once the raccoon was up in the tree, Mom would keep it pinned with the torch until Dick had shot it dead. By this time I was quite a good shot myself and would beg Dick to let me have a go at killing the raccoon but he would never entertain that idea in the slightest.

'If you shoot badly you'll injure the raccoon instead of doing a clean kill. An injured animal is dangerous; it will come down that tree and attack you!'

So I continued to shoot at tin cans, bottles and wooden targets in lieu... and wondered what was the point of becoming a good marksman if I would never be allowed to aim at a live target. Never once do I remember considering how I would feel if I did intentionally shoot and kill an animal. However, all too soon, I would find out what it felt like to take a life but I would be using my bare hands instead of a bullet.

2007 - The scuttling sounds grew louder drawing me back from my memories. They definitely did not sound like the scurrying rodent type sounds I remembered from my childhood. Chris was still clattering around downstairs, coaxing and wheedling the cats towards our bedroom. I reached over and flicked on his bedside table lamp and looked down at the floor. My eyes went straight to the large hole under our radiator, nope, no head poking out. Looked to my left and there was a very large black and grey moth. The wings were pounding against the floor boards with a scrabbling scuttling sound! Mystery solved. I managed to lure Chris back to bed after I had deposited the moth gently outside. The cats spent the rest of the night wide awake and made sure to come and bother us each time we fell asleep. Karma? You betcha!

The shoe tree

The shoe tree appeared as if by magic. Oh I don't mean the tree itself that had been in the exact same spot for a number of years. The shoes, however, seemed to cover it in a matter of days. Unmatched tatty shoes, boots and fluttering ribbons hanging from its branches. To this day no one knows who did it or why. It has simply become part of the local folklore, one of the unexplained oddities of the Island.

Word of the shoe tree spread quickly round the four main communities on the Island. These were comprised of; the Christians who were ensconced in their large acreage that ran along one of the lakes, the hippies who were dotted wherever they settled long enough to build shelter (with varying degrees of success), the wealthy resort owners who lived in some the best waterfront areas along the edge of the Island and the Indians who lived close to the lighthouse on their reserve at the far end of the Island.

At the opposite end of the Island was where the shoe tree displayed its footwear, draped off its branches like gaudy costume jewellery. The majority of Islanders couldn't get to it by foot as it was so far away from the main communities. In fact it grew along the side of a dirt road, 9 miles from the nearest modern convenience. No electricity or piped in water existed this far out on the Island. There were, however, a few hardy souls who set up home in the peace accessible via this road. Everyone else took an opportunity to admire the shoe tree when they ventured out to this end of the Island to swim in the lake which could be spotted shimmering a mile beyond the shoes.

I adored the quiet which grew in intensity as the dust billowed from the car wheels. I made myself listen beyond the crunching of the tires on small stones which were scattered along the road. I wish I could focus to this extent now but alas any background noise is intensely distracting and grows worse as I age. I have been assured that my hearing is within normal limits... When asked why I have concerns about my hearing, I struggle to explain the sense of loss I now experience when I realise I can no longer focus on specific sounds or on the intensity of silence.

When my father returned to the Island, he bought several acres of uncleared woodland beyond the shoe tree and he remains there to this day. There is still no electricity in his part of the Island and the running water has been plumbed in from one of his two wells. When I am not there, my mouth misses the flavour of that water. I do visit, though not as frequently or for as long as I wish to. I enjoy spending time near my father but that is not my only reason for visiting. When I am lucky enough to be there, I spend a lot of time wandering his land and trying to listen beyond the sound to the breeze shaking the pine boughs and making the needles rustle.

My father grows Bonsai's, feeds hummingbirds, encourages blackberry brambles to grow around a supporting frame instead of ripping their roots from the soil beneath, appreciating their bounty instead of fearing they will take over the garden like the weed they are. He predominantly favours Buddhist principles. Every once in a while, when standing on my favourite spot on his land, I hear the sound of silence and it is as magical as it was when I was still a wild hippie child. My father's land is my place of peace.

Liar, liar, pants on fire

My son is beginning to use harsh words as jagged edged weapons. I guess all children do this at his age but I find him using these word particularly disturbing because they remind me of a time in my life when these words featured strongly in my vocabulary.

Mom and Dick were away on holiday. They'd gone to England to visit my great grandmother and Dick's sons. I was staying with a woman called Faye, whom I disliked intensely but I felt vulnerable left in her care and desperately wanted her to be kind to me and for her to like me. So I did my best to win her affections with bright chatter and a pleasant manner; this was a huge effort for me and one which was not appreciated. I was not successful even once that I can remember. Several times after receiving an abrupt retort from Faye, I held her cat in my arms and cried silently into its fur. I also do not remember where my brother was; he may have been at the same place as I or perhaps he was lucky enough to be staying in my aunt's cramped little trailer during Mom's absence.

I would sit alone in her front room and stare out the window, wishing time away; wishing I was a grown up and no longer had to remain in the presence of people I despised. I spent a lot of my early adult years running away from people and situations, as and when it suited me. The freedom felt as good as I'd imagined; additively, falsely, empowering.

I could see the school from the front window of Faye's house. I had trouble deciding which building I hated more. I knew if I had to go back into the school building, it would kill me, I'd just die! So after lunch I walked along the perimeter of the school to the area where trees edged the boundaries facing my classroom. I went to a pine tree that had branches I knew would support my weight and I climbed till I thought I was high enough to be out of sight.

I watched the class from my perch, my vision blurred with unshed tears, my eyes fixed on the meanest girl in school; Rachel, the one who had humiliated me as a joke earlier that day. When she had passed me the note, I'd looked over at her, wondering who she wanted me to give it to. She'd answered by grinning and pointing at me. I opened the note.

'Look at Sally's clothes! Does she think she is the Queen of England or what?'

I hadn't noticed anything wrong with Sally's clothes. I looked closely at them, trying to think of a suitable rejoinder to write. Nope, no luck, I thought she looked quite nice actually!

'Well LaDeDah!' I wrote hoping that would suffice and keep Rachel interested in passing me more notes. She didn't make eye contact again, so I guessed I had written the wrong thing. I found out exactly how wrong as we left class for lunch.

I felt a pinch on my arm as Sally and Rachel walked past.

'Hey fleabag, you gotta lotta nerve calling me a show off!' hissed Sally.

'I didn't'...

'Liar, liar, pants on fire; Rachel showed me what you wrote!'

Well then why wasn't Sally mad at Rachel? Why was everything so confusing?

Embarrassed, I went to Faye's for lunch. I asked Faye why Sally wasn't mad at Rachel.

'It doesn't matter why, you shouldn't have written mean things about Sally! No wonder you have no friends!'

She turned her back to me to serve the food. Through my silent tears I could see that her hair fell down her back in a shinning brown sheet, all except one strand that had caught on her top. I reached out to disengage the trapped hair, wanting to help her, to make her like me.

It must have pulled against her scalp because she flung herself round and shouted ' and now you pull my hair while my back is turned? What is the matter with you?!'

Shocked I just stared at her instead of trying to explain that I was trying to make her hair a matching shinning sheet with no hair out of place.

'You can go without lunch and see if that improves your temper! I'll be glad to hand you back to your mother.'

I sat on the couch, trying to think of ways to pinch Faye and make it look like an accident! I sucked my thumb (yes I still did that and for many years to come) and smoothed her purring cat. I listened to Faye chew and swallow while I stared at the hated school, until at long last the lunch break was over and I was able to go hide in the tree.

Bright spark

I pressed my cheek onto the smooth bark of the Alder tree, wrapped my arms round the trunk and sighed. It was the tallest tree on the property and the branch I sat on was higher than the roof of the house. The branches were evenly spaced round the trunk and easy to climb, once I had figured out how to swing myself up onto the lowest branch.

The tree was in full leaf but I could see most everything I wanted to from the branch I sat on. To my far left I could see the roof of a house but no longer could I see the roof of the garage that used to be behind it. The reason for this was that I had burnt it down last week. I had offered to clear Mrs Hayward's yard to earn a bit of spending money.

The yard was large and the grass on her lawn was dried brown already. She was old and didn't spend a lot of time tending to her lawn and so by mid July, it had lost its battle with the sun. The task of clearing all that grass by raking as she had requested seemed ridiculous and insurmountable to my 12 year old mind. The crispy blades slipped through the tines of the rake, leaving me frustrated in a very short time. I tried to pull up the grass by hand but soon realised that would take even longer! Then I remembered that I had seen a cigarette lighter on the table in the porch and proceeded to use that to burn the offending grass away.

At first this idea worked remarkably well, I would light small patches and then stamp them out as the flames burned down close to the ground. I left the small circular patches dotted round her lawn as I worked my way round the back of the house. The grass around the garage was longer and a gust of wind fanned the flames upwards. To my horror the bottom of one garage wall caught fire!

'Help, help, there's a fire out here'! I shouted towards the house feeling frantic with fear.

'What dear?' Mrs Hayward peered out at the spreading fire. 'Oh that'll burn itself out in no time.'

As she spoke, the breeze swept the fire onto the garage roof. The two of us walked to safety at end of her driveway and watched as the neighbours put out the fire, but not before it had mostly spent itself by eating through the garage roof. Mrs Hayward insisted on paying me, which only added to my shame. In a small community such as ours, news spreads almost as fast as grass fires and by that evening everyone knew what I had done. The neighbourhood kids delighted in this further evidence of my weirdness.

'Here comes the fire starting fleabag! Didja steal the matches from your hippie dad?' they shrieked in that gleeful, slightly hysterical voice linked with bullying. The cruel words flickered from child to child, in much the same manner as the fire had spread from dried lawn to timber garage.

'It was a lighter, not matches', I spat back, thus sealing my fate as the class freak with that ridiculous retort. I left before they could tease me anymore and climbed up my Alder tree to sit in quiet peaceful solitude. Luckily, it was only part way through the long hot summer, I didn't have to spend time with the other kids if I chose not to and my life was about to get a whole lot more interesting. Dick had decided that we were going to get some bunnies!

A tale of two (who quickly became more than a few) rabbits

'Bunnies!' I grabbed my brother's hands and danced round in gleeful circles until he fell over. I lay beside him on the grass and watched the clouds waft past as I imagined how it would feel to smooth the fur of a rabbit. Last winter, Dick had decided that we would begin rearing our own meat. We had begun with some of our chickens who had stopped laying.

The chicks and roosters from that year would follow me around clucking and burbling amongst themselves while I got on with my chores in the yard. They were allowed to be free range as long as someone was with them for protection. The young roosters would try to crow, usually getting halfway trough the vocalisation before stopping suddenly as if they'd forgotten the script. Unable to resist, I began to mimic them and my crow matured in progression with theirs until I too had mastered the music of an adult rooster's crow. I can crow like a rooster to this day, one of my multitude of useless skills that I acquired simply because I could.

The two rabbits that we would use as breeders were being delivered today. Dick had built a very large hutch for them and told me it would be my job to clean it out and to pick fresh greens for them each day. I was used to helping clean the chicken coop so this didn't bother me and the idea of picking clover and dandelion as a treat for them each morning and evening sounded like fun...until Dick showed me the size of the bucket he expected me to fill! It was huge and reached from the ground to the top of my thigh. I was 5 foot 6inches tall already so that should give you some idea of how big the bucket was. Luckily our property was large, the fresh greens were easily accessible and it only took me about half an hour to fill the bucket twice a day. Watching the rabbits enjoy this treat was more than worth the work and I only sulked while collecting fresh greens if I was feeling cross about something else.

As well as their large hutch which had two complete living areas, Dick had also built a wire frame that they could be placed in. This gave them the opportunity to graze on the tall grasses which lined the bordering ditch along our driveway. I thought this seemed a great freedom for the cage born rabbits and loved to watch them frolicking inside the frame, racing the length of it and flicking their legs sideways as they shot past each other, till at last they flopped onto their sides panting with exhaustion. They especially loved to lie in holes they had dug in the ground. I imagined them to be trying to cover up their half dug escape routes with their bodies, a fanciful notion no doubt inspired by having recently read Watership Down by Richard Adams.

They also spent a lot of time working at making baby bunnies (an act that was over before it could even begin to be interesting) and in no time at all I was watching with fascination as the first litter made their mother's fur ripple as they kicked and squirmed inside her. Their movements were more clearly visible as the end of the pregnancy approached and on rare occasions she would allow me to place my hand flat against her side while I tried to count the number of babies. This was my first experience of midwifery. Many years in the future I would perform abdominal examinations on a daily basis and the magic of feeling a living being move inside someone has never lessened. To be allowed to do so is a privilege.

Survival of the 'unthinkingest'

Soon the Dame began to rip out chunks of fur from the thickening ruff that lined her neck. She placed these in her straw bedding. Dick said she this was a sign that the birth was approaching. She became reluctant to allow me to touch her and would stamp her feet in warning when I cleaned out her hutch and dart her head at me if I tried to clean her sleeping area. Fluffy bunnies can actually be scary...

One morning when I went out to feed the rabbits their greens I couldn't see them anywhere. Usually they waited for me in the larger part of their hutch, lurking with intent to begin eating. I looked inside and saw Ziggy (the Sire) crouched over strips of white, his mouth busy chewing. I looked closer and saw that his chin was wet and red...blood! Where had blood come from?

'Dick? Mom!' I shrieked and my stomach felt cold and hard.

Dick ran out, rubber boots on his feet and mom followed close behind, speeding up to pass Dick when she saw the look on my face. I grabbed her hand and shoved it in Ziggy's direction.

'What is he doing?'

'Fuck me gently!' Dick kicked the leg of the hutch and Ziggy jumped away from his feast.

'Whuh...why is he eating meat? How did he get meat?' My voice trailed off to a whisper as I realised that I was looking at an impossibly tiny rabbit ear which was attached to an equally small head. This was horrible, I must be imagining, dreaming, it wasn't real!

'We know to separate them earlier next time, eh?' Dick flung a look in mom's direction.

'Are there any left?' Mom's voice caught on the edge of hope. I half listened still absorbed by the sight of that tiny ear, smaller than my baby finger nail and wondered what was to become of it now.

'Two that I can see but she's in there with them so could be more!' Dick picked Ziggy up by the scruff of his neck, gently placed him in the far end of the hutch and slid the divider in to keep him from indulging any further cannibalistic urges.

Days passed. I learned to accept that it was natural for male rabbits to eat their young so that the female would quickly develop renewed urges to breed again. I forgave him and began to enjoy having his undivided attention while his mate was occupied with raising their babies. I played with him and fed him bananas as a special treat once week. Smoothed his ears against my top lip. Spent golden moments in the sunshine; holding him against my chest while I smoothed his ears against my top lip.

Eventually the babies emerged from their nest. They were so tiny and the most adorable things I had ever seen. Soon their mom let me hold them, little scraps of warmth and softness in the palm of my hand. Dick was delighted to see that there were seven of them.

'That's seven home-grown meals for the winter!' He rubbed his stomach and grinned.

'I was very disturbed at the thought of eating these bundles of velvety fur! 'We can't eat them; they are too tiny and too cute!'

Dick sighed. 'I told you that we would be raising them for meat! I told you not to get attached to them! Anyway, they won't be so cute in a few months time when it is time to kill them!' he said matter of factly, as if that statement should resolve any lingering issues I might have.

I knew Dick meant what he said and so I didn't get attached to them after that and they did get bigger and a lot less cute. The idea of eating them didn't bother me as much any more but the fact that he expected me to kill them, did! My only experience with killing our livestock so far had been the chickens last winter and it was an experience I would prefer to never repeat.

I was made to watch and learn as Dick picked up a chicken upside down and expertly placed a finger on either side of the neck swiftly sliding his fingers towards the head and breaking the neck as he did so. He placed the chicken on the ground where it lay lifeless.

'Not duin it!' I muttered and backed away.

'Okay then, to save time, I will have to kill them all like this!' with that Dick picked up the next chicken, placed it on a stump of wood and chopped it's head off with the axe. The chicken then got off the stump and ran headless around the yard, frantically flapping it's wings until at last it collapsed in a heap.

'Up to you...help the chickens have a peaceful end or be responsible for them dying in fear?'

Resigned, I picked up a chicken trying not to look at her trusting eyes. She had followed me round the yard as a chick. I had always been kind to her. In my haste to get the deed over with I pulled too hard as I slid my fingers down her neck...so hard that I tore her head right off. Her demise taints my memory of her.

It would be different with the rabbits Dick assured me, they were to be killed in a different way. Hang them from your hand by their feet and follow with a swift karate style chop to the back of their neck. He was right in a way. The rabbits seemed to die without a struggle, calm from the moment they were suspended from my hand. However, their calmness didn't make me feel any better... death is still death! We ate well that winter, in fact I grew over a foot in height by spring but I had to chew each mouthful with a closed mind.

Survival of the unthinkingest...

Meadowlark's hidden treasures

Head down but not watching where I was going, I stumbled often but had, so far, managed not to fall head first into the very substance I was following. Meadowlark's droppings were increasing in frequency and in quantity, what was going on?

Meadowlark was our very fragrant, somewhat odious goat but I loved her all the same. She started off living on a small acreage across the road from us. I used to cut through the back of Tony's to get to where the horses grazed. (He owned a store full of other people's cast offs, furniture, bric a brak, clothing, books and everything in that place was an endless source of fascination for me.) I loved to smooth the horses' incredibly soft noses. Spending quiet time watching them graze, while the hot sun baked the back of my neck and the dusty air tickled my nose, made me feel that all was well in my world.

Then one day a brown and white goat bleated at me from a fenced off area to the right. She stood on her hind legs, supporting herself on the fence with her front hooves and greedily absorbed all the attention I could give her. The sun was behind her, beginning to set but still bright and it lit her up as if she was a firework; like a clear version of the halo effect that appears around a street light when you squint your eyes.

I fell in love with her that day and spent most of the evening talking about her. I went straight from school each day to visit her until one day I went to see her and she was gone. The man who owned her came out and told me he'd sold her and I trailed home feeling flat. Guess who was bleating at me from the back of our big red truck when I arrived?!

She settled into our lives and we into hers, with ease. Dick had plans to milk her instead of buying cow's milk. The dropping trail day I was writing about at the beginning of this, was the day that Dick realised Meadow Lark had become more than he had bargained for! However, he turned out to have got the better end of the deal... Still following the clues left by Meadow Lark I became aware that I could hear her bleating in what can only be described as an undertone and as I neared the shade under my favourite tree I could see her lying on her side, panting.

She grunted, to greet me, I thought and then from her bottom appeared a face framed by a pair of tiny hooves! Not sure what to do, I crept to her head and smoothed her face along the side of her nose. She liked that and rested her head in my lap for a few moments until the urge to push came upon her once again. As she strained, her head lifted from my lap and she bleated and her tongue flickered in and out. I knelt up and watched in fascination as her baby inched forward while she pushed, stopping its progress as Meadow Lark tired.

Hearing the front door of our house open, I looked in that direction and saw mom. I picked up a stone and threw it towards the house, waving my arms frantically as the noise made her look in my direction and then beckoning her towards me. She came quickly towards me, likely with a sense of dread because I was on the ground, non verbal and not mobile. When she was near enough I pointed to the baby and as if my finger was the missing instruction, the very wet baby slithered out onto the ground. I had been with Meadow Lark for no more than 20 minutes but it felt as if days had passed. Mom held me as I cried.

When I had regained my composure, mum turned me towards Meadow Lark and to my amazement the little baby goat was already on it's feet with it's fur bristling out in many directions just like her mother's, except for the spot that Meadow Lark was still licking. The baby started to stand and turn around but collapsed in a jumbled heap of its legs. I giggled and then made my way carefully around the baby so that I could stroke Meadow Lark. Mom busied herself with picking some Comfrey to feed Meadow Lark, it was to help bring on the after birth and to speed healing she said. She had done the same thing with our rabbit and judging by the speed with which she ate the Comfrey it was a tasty treat as well.

Meadow Lark grunted in that tone that was now familiar to me, she was pushing again. Mom and I looked and something bulged at the opening of her vagina. It was wet fur instead of the placenta mom had expected and she rushed over to Meadow Lark and encouraged her to stand.
    'I need gravity to help get this baby out before the Comfrey takes effect!' mom panted, holding Meadow Lark's head.

    'Why?' I kept my eye on the progress at the opposite end from where my mom was.
    'It makes the womb contract and then the opening to the womb will close which means the baby will get stuck.'
    Oh please Meadow, push, I thought, concentrating all my hope on her soon to be stuck baby.

Meadow Lark pushed and pushed and mom gave me her head and went to pull on the baby in time with her contractions until at last the 2nd baby was on the ground.

Meadow Lark lay down, resting her head on my legs until Mom said, 'Nudge her head round to the baby, she has to lick it clean so she can get to know it.'

I nudged her, she licked, the baby bleated and then staggered to its feet. Both babies then began to bang her udder with their heads until Meadow Lark stood to allow them to feed. I refused to leave them to eat my own supper so mom left me to my vigil until I was driven into the house by the night's chill. That night I floated to sleep cradled on the memories of the day. Sometimes I still do...

Ode to Lennie

John Steinbeck's novel Of Mice and Men was required reading at school. I adored the book and really felt stirrings of empathy for Lennie. I now realise that he was probably autistic and this may be why I felt connected to his character. He made mistakes but for all the right reasons, at least in his opinion. We were supposed to write an essay of sorts about the book but instead I wrote and submitted this poem. I got an A+!

Ode to Lennie
Growing up slow
You try so hard
Small dreams and you glow

You're playing all your cards
Mice in your pocket
Nice to pet
Angry bitten fingers
Crushed little head

His voice rises and falls
Telling you not to fail
Listen to the waterfall
And the sound of the thrashing quail

People say 'well done!'
You know you've done wrong
Fade away to think of a rabbit's brood
And to hear the bird's soft song

Thinking of soft nices

You laugh
Curley turns and slices
You
With his wrath...

Fear beats into you
Voices...people screaming
This horror you must undo
Crush that hand
Your tears are streaming

Soft...
Grown up so slow
You've tired so hard
You've played all your cards

Golden head and dress
All curls and twirls
Now she's a mess
That soft pretty girl

Running by the stream bank
Memory's clear now
Falling..the ground is dank
Going over old vows

Pains going
You smile
And leave this life behind...

Golden memories of caramel coloured sand

My brother and I loved to swim. We were always active but mom had no trouble keeping us amused in the summer. All she had to do was take us to the 'Spit' and we would spend all day in or on top of the water. The 'Spit' is a finger of land surrounded by water, one side was an inlet and had warm water and a sandy beach a few miles long and the other had varying sizes of stones underfoot and faced the Atlantic; great for rock pools full of interesting creatures but no good for safe swimming! One side of the beach was made up of fine caramel coloured sand and covered in driftwood.

Mom would check the tide tables to make sure we'd get there at high tide. As soon as she stopped the car we would race over to the sand and carefully choose a manoeuvrable log which we would slide from side to side down the sand until it got deep enough into the water and began to float. On we would hop and spend the majority of our time on top of it in the water, leaping off to swim and then back on to dry off in the heat.

Lying belly down on our wooden floats, we could watch the sea creatures pass deep underneath us. Most often we would see fish but very occasionally a sting ray would fly by or we'd catch glimpses of jelly fish drifting along on the undercurrent. There were frequent flashes of white as we passed rocks laden with barnacles; we took careful note of those rocks, for when the tide lowered we were likely to be walking on that barnacled sea bed as we made our way into the water to swim. The salt crystals itched as they dried on our skin, leaving snowflake designs to be admired and then brushed away.

Once or twice during the day we would make our way back to the beach and drowse on our towels for a while. Sleeping in the sun is still one of my most favourite sensations; I adore that feeling of sleepy serenity that comes with the blanket of heat. We never wore sunscreen in those days, I'd never even heard of it. I only remember burning once though and that was when we were in California. I had shaved my legs for the first time, without permission and only on my shin bones. I was too scared to turn over and lie on my back while sunbathing, so I spent the entire day on my front while my back crisped and began to blister.

I suppose we must have had lunch but all I remember is the BBQ's. Towards the end of the day Mom would call us to come and eat. She often made BBQ's salmon stuffed with fresh dill, onions and lemon. My mom had a way of BBQ'ing most things though and some of my favourites were BBQ's potatoes, sliced most of the way through and then slices of onion and tabs of butter placed between ach slice before wrapping the potato in foil and cooking it in the coals. BBQ'd corn on the cob was sweet and simple to prepare by wrapping the corn husks, which had been soaked in water, back around the corn cob before placing it on the grill. We always had raw vegetables too, cucumbers, carrots, celery, tomatoes as well as huge watermelons and/or strawberries, peaches and cherries.

My brother and I would eat for what felt like hours (but was probably only minutes) before going back to the sand to beach comb and look in the rock pools for interesting creatures until our food had processed for mom deemed to be a suitable amount of time. Then we would head back into the water, growing increasingly chilly as the sun dropped in the sky. Eventually we'd get dried off and dressed and warm up while toasting marshmallows over the embers so of the wood stoked BBQ pit. Those days were glorious and it is one of the few episodes of my childhood that I would willingly live again

A trip to the tip

Occasionally, on a summer morning, I would bicycle to the tip with a packed lunch stashed in a bucket slung on the handlebars. It was down the road from our property, about a mile or so away, just before the graveyard on the opposite side of the road. It wasn't the type of place where leftover consumables were left. This was more the rubbish heap equivalent of beach combing for there was all manner of unwanted household items slung on top of each other until they resembled surreal hillocks. Many of them were still perfectly serviceable once introduced to some soap, water and elbow grease. Other items needed the former treatment and a dash of ingenuity to enhance them.

I would set off from home at first light, when the dew anointed the grass blades. It wasn't that I had far to travel but more that I could not sleep for my desire to already be there. I would spend hours rummaging round this treasure trove. I once unearthed a whole set of bone handled steak knives and proudly brought them home. Much to my delight we used them for years after.

It wasn't the safest place for a clumsy child to be. Looking back now I wonder how I made it to adulthood without a broken bone or worse. I had no innate awareness of danger. The mounds of discarded appliances and brick a brack were unsteady and a carelessly placed foot would cause a mini avalanche. I once ended up on the ground with my foot in the bucket I used for carting around my finds, an empty frame on my wrist and a sore hip. I brought the frame home that afternoon, slung rakishly round my neck and over one shoulder, the edge of the frame hit my right thigh on each upward stroke of the pedal, adding another bruise to my collection for that day.

I loved the feel of the sun warming me as the hours lengthened and found the noises of the wild creatures quite soothing. I don't remember any of them being scared of me or vice versa. Rats wombled around, disappearing under the piles and emerging ahead or to one side and snakes sometimes made an appearance, languidly winding their way through the dried grass that bordered the dirt floored tip. Fat bees bumbled their way around flower heads while the crickets thundered their way through their concerts always finishing with the same crescendo which then crashed into absolute but momentary silence before their music began once again to spiral up through the same gleeful composition. My absolute favourite tip companion was a crow who followed me about (I am certain it was always the same one as he had a missing toe on the right), tilting his head from side to side as he watched me.

Occasionally a cart horse called Zed would wander up to the fence at the back and whicker at me for some attention. If there were apples on the tree, I would give him a few or else grab handfuls of sweet grass that grew in the shade and giggle as his lips made 'flub flub' sounds while he worked the grass into his mouth. I used to visit Zed's owner, Ernie as he liked my company and would show me how to muck out his Zed's and let me finish the job off by flicking pitchfork fulls of perfumed hay over the floor. In the winter he'd make something he called 'hot mash' for the horse which smelt a bit like old beer bottles. Zed ate it with gusto so it must have tasted better than it smelt! Once he gave me a dill pickle and told me to offer it to Zed. I did and proceeded to laugh my stomach hurt and no noise came out as I watched him eat the pickle with his lips raised so high that all his teeth were exposed. To this day I do not know if Zed enjoyed the pickle or if he realised he'd made a mistake too late to spit the offending article out.

Some days I would take a detour on my way home from Ernie's or the tip by making a stop at the small grave yard to wander along the rows reading the inscriptions on the tombstones. It was shady, cool, oh so quiet in this bone yard and utterly peaceful. I never once saw anyone else there...which made me wonder what was the point of burying the remains of those who had moved on?

Tadpoles and Players lights.

Our elementary school was bordered around the back and halfway down both sides by forest. If you stood with your back to the school, the left hand side went back for miles and was full of trails through which deer roamed at night; the right hand side had a much shallower bit of woodland and a few hundred feet in led you to the local hairdresser's house. She ran her business in her home so she knew if we went onto her property and would come out and shout from her porch.

'Hey, you kids! Get back to school!'

Of course that just encouraged them. It got so they'd make as much noise as possible while running full tilt towards her property, in the hopes of being the one who could get her to shout the loudest. There was no popularity contest with this game, every kid, including me, got to join in if they wanted. I still lurked on the peripheries though; the game was too noisy and like most playground activities, a bit too pointless. I would creep up the sides of the path in order to get close enough to see her face when she came out to shout at us and would wonder if it was healthy for her face to go that shade of red.

Between the end of the school field and the start of the forest was a stream that ran the length of the property and beyond. The water was cold, clear and tasty. This was back in the days when kids drank from streams, wiped dirt from freshly uprooted carrots on their jeans before eating them, ate fruit without washing it, played in or near running streams and took candy from strangers; all without having to suffer being told the horror stories of children who had done the same and who had come to a painful end.

The stream was a constant source of interest for me. I loved the way the running water washed the moss on the underwater rocks and made the fronds stream out like green hair. In the spring, frog spawn occupied me for weeks. I once brought it home in a huge gallon jar once but mom made me take it straight back to the stream. She said there was no need to take it from the wild when I could walk to it in less than 5 minutes and see it in its natural habitat. She was right, of course. Lesson learned.

I had begun babysitting earlier the year before for a bit of cash and I do mean 'a bit'. I think I made about 25 cents and hour or less! Nowadays I make sure to get our youngest son to bed before going out and we pay a decent babysitter £5.00 an hour to do no more than keep the couch warm and the TV company while he sleeps soundly...at least until we get home. Why do children never wake until parents come home? I swear our youngest has an internal alcohol detector which he turns on as he goes to sleep and then proceeds to wake throughout the night according to how much alcohol we've consumed. More than 2 glasses worth of wine fumes drifting through our happy heads and we can pretty much give up on the thought of a decent rest or much sleep!

I lost one of my babysitting jobs when I burnt down Mrs Hayward's garage. I actually was quite responsible when it came to caring for younger kids but I have no idea why the other set of parents trusted me to look after their children after the garage fiasco. Perhaps they were just desperate to go out. Their kids were nice although getting them to settle to sleep was always a challenge and I used to feel quite exhausted by the time I had. The more I looked after them the more I began to realise that having children of my own was not something I would be in any rush to do.

Once the children were asleep I would wander through the rest of the house inspecting everything they owned. I had no interest in watching TV, we didn't have one in our house and besides other people's real lives were so fascinating. Especially the paraphernalia hidden in the bedroom! Quite interesting those magazines and the stories sent in by readers, well! Did people do those kinds of things for real? Intriguing to the billionth degree! I wasn't quite sure what some of the equipment I found in the drawer was for but a thorough read of the magazines eventually provided explanations. I had heard my mom enjoying herself enough times and had thought my mom's interest in sex at the advanced age of 34 was abnormal. Now a somewhat sickening realisation began to emerge... all old people were enjoying sex and somehow that was twice as gross...eeeewwwww! Disgust at the debauchery of adults quenched the flickers of desire that had begun to emerge. I returned the magazines to their hiding place and turned my attention to the chest of drawers in the bedroom.

There was quite a large pile of folded money on top, $220 in total. I left it the way I had found it, with the back of the fold facing left and some bills hanging slightly out of the crease, like newly rebellious teenagers starting the search for their own identity. What had caught my eye was the carton of Players light cigarettes, open and missing a few packs. When I left that evening the carton was missing another. I am so relieved that they never noticed the missing pack as I am incapable of lying, except by direct omission and would have confessed immediately had they asked. This was not the best trait for a thief to be cursed with and luckily, the urge to steal something did not become a habit.

I had always been mesmerized by the act of smoking and to this day I will blatantly stare at smokers, my attention drawn in by their rituals. The bend of the wrist as the cigarette is placed between the lips. The way cheeks sink in with the force of inhaling, the squint of the eye for those who inhaled hands free and wished to avoid burning their eyes with the hot fumes. The way some people puffed out a cloud and others blew out a long plume.

Identical amongst all smokers was the glimmer of light that sparked in their eyes as the nicotine took effect. More than anything, I wanted to know what that glimmer felt like which was why I had taken a pack of cigarettes to experiment with. At the time it did not even cross my mind that it was tantamount to stealing and I would have been mortified had I been caught and then made to realise the significance of my action.

After several attempts I mastered the technique of placing flame to tip and simultaneously sucking at other end which is required to ignite a tube of tobacco. I was hooked from the moment I drew my first mouthful of smoke in. 12 years old, not yet inhaling the noxious smoke but already in love, love love with the feeling of nicotine kissing my brain. It mimicked the feeling I got from spinning but I was certain that smoking to get the heady effect made me look much cooler. Thus began a love affair which was to continue for the next 20 years and that still tries to lure me into its poisonous rapture 8 years after the last puff left my lungs.

Dancing Orcas

The island I grew up on was too small to warrant its own secondary school. Instead we took the ferry to the larger Island close by and were bussed up to the junior high school. Once we started going to this new school and mixing with people we hadn't gown up with, all the rules changed. Suddenly I was considered attractive by the boys, which made me popular with the girls, whom I mostly ignored in retaliation for the years of neglect that I had suffered at their hands. The flavour of power was exquisite.

We would traipse to the ferry in a school sized pack of noise makers and as soon as we boarded, us girls would leave the boys and pile into the toilets to apply make up. We had to rush to get it on before the ferry started up as the vibrations sent up from the motors made it difficult to apply our maquillage with the required steady hand. Once the ferry got out of dock the rolling action as it made its way across the choppy water, made any application, steady or otherwise, impossible!

Now this was the late 70's, when make up mimicked tropical plumage and like so many gaudy birds, we would remove it all during the ferry ride home before our parents saw it and passed comment. Old fogies...what did they know anyway? I have no daughters but still cringe at my stepson's girlfriend's makeup...no escape for the guilty I guess! I keep quiet though for I am sure any comment I make would have them thinking that I am far too old to know what I am talking about anyway and perhaps they are right! Life is an eternal circle...

I was lucky enough to grow up in a part of the world where I could watch family pods of Orcas at play. They would travel through the body of water that separated the Island we lived on from the larger Island on which our high school was located. The Orcas were not in any hurry, this pilgrimage was more of a holiday for them and they would stop frequently and loll about resting or playing.

Occasionally this would happen near the ferry's path and so it would have to stay in dock, engines off, until the Orcas had moved on. So not only did we get to marvel at the beauty of these huge beasts frolicking like children, we were also legitimately late for school. Bonus!

My friend crow

I can't remember where I found the injured young crow. All I recall is patiently working at calming him enough to gain his trust, getting closer until I could gather him up in my hands and bring him home to mom. His body cradled in my cupped hands, his heart beating against my fingers, his wing hanging limply over my right hand.

I gathered grubs, worms, grass seed and berries for him to eat, more each day it seemed. Mom had splinted his wing with Popsicles sticks in the folded closed position, replacing the splint each time he pecked it off, till one day he flapped his wing open and then closed.

'It's healed now' she said, sending a small smile in my direction, 'you'll have to say goodbye soon'.

'Why does he have to go mom? He is happy here with me, look!' I gestured to him standing on the sill of the open window, showing no signs of wanting to leave.

'He is a wild thing and needs to be with his own kind', she said gently.

My eyes brimmed with tears and I looked away from the softness that had appeared around her eyes as she spoke.

My friend crow loved to ride around on my shoulder and caw softly at me, looking expectantly at my face until I cawed back. Satisfied, he would hop off my shoulder onto anything of a suitable height and wander around, always keep an eye out for our cat. Sure enough, several days later, he hopped from the window onto the slope of the conservatory roof, and then leapt into the air, flapping his wings frantically until he caught an updraft and soared out of sight. I sat and stared at the empty sky, tears falling silently onto the smooth surface of Dick's studio counter.

Dusk began to fall and still I sat and stared, eyes dry and burning now, stomach churning, bladder growing uncomfortably full. I was determined to triumph at this challenge of endurance moroseness. Then the mosquitoes began to bite as the temperature dropped and I grudgingly reached over to slide the screen across the window frame. As I turned to go down to the toilet, I saw a shadow land on the conservatory roof and then make its way to the window. Before he could tap on the screen, I had flung it open, welcoming my friend crow back into the house, along with a fresh swarm of biting, buzzing nightmares.

I gave him a stern look and said 'I am going for a pee, waited all day y'ano!' my voice betrayed me by quavering on the last word. He wasn't fooled by my peevishness and ignoring my petulant tone, he began to hop and snap at the air. My friend crow was hungry and he could hear the dinner bell pealing in a series of minuscule top pitched notes. My issues were not his concern, a lesson I would learn time and time again as I blundered through this life.

Breaking point

Such a sweet young girl,
Everyone used to say,
But someone's going to pay,
Such a sweet young girl...

Into this world she came,
Mother's still a child,
Her hairs' all curls, such a shame,
Unyielding and wild...

So young and not ready,
For wild parties at night,
I brought my Chewie,
To stand naked under the flashing lights...

Standing in the doorway,
We try to understand,
Nakedness that way,
The moving of the hand...

Such a sweet young girl,
Everyone used to say,
Look at her dress twirl,
As she goes about her play...

A man waits silently,
As she runs down the street,
He leaps out giantly,
And throws her off her feet...

Hard sidewalk,

Cold beneath her back,
Bad man's talk,
Her mind goes off track...

Confused and mixed up,
Today she swallowed,
Lots of pills...what a thrill...

On the day I woke up
I felt so hollow...

I realised that I had reached breaking point as I wrote the poem above on the day after I tried to kill myself. No longer could I endure Dick's abuse or it would kill me by proxy and I wasn't about to allow myself to sink to that depth of despair again. So when Dick left to travel down the large Island on an overnight trip, I told mom that if she didn't leave him, I was going to tell him I was pregnant so he would kick me out. I wasn't pregnant but I was willing to lie. Mom instinctively knew I wasn't and asked me why I would say such a thing. So I told her everything.

There is no need to describe it all here. The story has been told many a time before by other survivors of abuse and the deliberate act of trying to destroy someone's soul is equally damaging for every victim. Whether the abuse is dressed up as a religious war, called ethnic cleansing, or described by paedophiles as the lure of Lolita; the end result is the same, varying degrees of destruction. What also varies is the support given after the abuse ends. Some are abandoned and some lucky enough to be loved long enough to heal up their wounds with scars thick enough to hold the pain at bay.

When Dick phoned that night mom told him that she wanted him to stay away for a few days and then we walked across the 12 foot wide ditch that bordered our property with the Police Station and the police chief's home. I told the chief everything I could and the look in his eyes and sadness in his voice when he called me 'Cupcake' was awful to see and made me forgot my fear at what Dick was going to do to me for telling on him. Looking back now I can imagine the chief's shock at learning the extent of the madness that went on next door to his home. I wonder if it made him feel less of a man to know that he couldn't protect a little girl who lived close enough to speak to on a daily basis. He was kind enough to stop himself from asking me why I had not come to him years ago.

To a degree, I had already learnt to compartmentalise disturbing incidents restraining them behind firewalls in my mind. With help, I began gathering up these particular experiences, gave them a good dousing down to put out the harmful flames and then wrapped them up gently before I stored them away a in a protected part of my mind. It is a bit lonely for them there as I don't visit. Other survivors have a need to take their memories out and air them but I think it is best not to in my case as there is no telling what kind of damage mine would get up to if let loose after all this time.

In hindsight I am amazed that we were able to benefit from the support provided by a wonderful woman named Brenda Knight. Back in those days claims of abuse had to be substantiated by witnesses. Of course the madness that lived inside Dick was much too calculating for that and there were never any witnesses, even my mom hadn't know what he was up to. I do know that mom had to go to court and that although Dick was not jailed for his abuse he was ordered to pay for a psychologist for myself, my brother and my mom. The court proceedings took several months and during this time I became quite angry with mom for not sensing what he had done to me for the years we had lived with Dick, how could she have not noticed I asked myself? After all I had told her about the 'French kiss', she had seen the 'painted panties'. All too soon I would have an understanding of exactly how she could have genuinely been blissfully unaware of the extent of the abuse and to this day I am angry with myself for my inobservance.

The psychologist was Brenda. She specialised in working with victims of abuse and later wrote a book called 'Am I the only one?' which included individual stories from children she had supported. That was my first experience of being published. She signed my copy in 1985 with this message: *'Dear Denyse, to a great young woman who deserves only the best and will achieve it. Love Brenda'*. If I had stayed with her a few more years she may have discovered that there was another reason for many of behaviours but my future diagnosis did not even achieve classification until the late 1980's. I do wonder how my life may have been altered if I could have received help with what I know is a disability. I also wonder if I would wish the next 23 years of my life to have been greatly different. I'll tell you the most significant bits as this book goes on.

My brother also had a story in her book. My brother, the person I adored more than my own ability to breathe and I had no idea that Dick had leashed him up and made him crawl around the conservatory like a puppy dog. That was the least of my brother's story and I can not forgive myself for not protecting him. I have forgiven my mother for not seeing what was happening to me but can not give myself the same absolution. I had no excuse you see, it was happening to me too and I should have seen the signs, the change in his behaviour. We both went from sunny children to sullen shadows. Once I knew how unobservant I had been I made a decision that I would never have a child of my own, how could I risk it? In my heart I knew I was not worthy of the privilege of being able to nurture and protect a child. Perhaps if I could apologise to Jia for not protecting him, I could begin to forgive myself.

To explain the reason why I can not, I need to take you from this point of my life into the future. In my late 20's, after a series of disastrous relationships (being in a relationship is challenge at the best of times but imagine living with someone like me who is easily distracted by the wonders of their own world and you'll get an idea of why none of my boyfriends stuck around) and failed jobs, I ended up in England and began training as a midwife.

Hearing the song Jaya Govinda by Kula Shaker coming from the radio for the first time, I became quietly and overwhelmingly convinced that I had lost my mind in a spectacular though not unpleasant fashion. My brother's first and middle name was Jia Govinda and I had recently returned from his memorial ceremony! I thought that my grief had tipped me over into auditory hallucinations. Luckily I was wrong, it was just one of those strange karmic occurrences that life throws my way to trip me up on occasion!

Jia shared with me some of the most momentous and life changing experiences, not all of them were good but I felt these burdens were halved by the fact that they were shared. He was the only person who could qualify the significance and authenticity of these shared experiences. Although I thought the burden was halved, I don't know what he thought about this, we didn't talk about these experiences. Now I wish we had. I have learned from this, I know I need to ask people how they feel, to not just assume. I know I should, but I do not often do this... I live so wrapped up in my own world, with so much going on in my mind, that there is sometimes no room for other's feelings.

The day I learned of his death was one that had begun with a new life. I had helped a woman birth her baby for the first time and was ecstatic, riding high on the endorphin rush of this privileged, magical experience, only to come down with a huge crash when the phone rang at 10pm. I forgot about the miracle of birth, got seriously drunk on whiskey (which I hate but it was the only hard liquor in the house) and spent hours trying to convince myself that it was all a horrible mistake and that I would soon be told Jia was alive and well.

The next day I booked plane tickets to travel to Canada. The trip was hellish, the plane seemed filled with young men who freakishly resembled my brother. The cabin crew were remarkably kind and understanding and helped me to move seats a few times to escape the mind boggling experience. I arrived in Canada, exhausted from 26 hours travelling in a hollow limbo. This new reality was all wrong, for it did not include my brother.

My auntie Carol came to my rescue yet again and collected me from the airport and we went directly to the funeral home where the rest of my family had gathered. I hadn't seen my brother for six years and in that time he had grown from lanky teenager to a young man. I spent considerable time in the funeral parlour approaching his lifeless body by increments, drawn by the size of his hands and determined to see them close up; to make that my final image of him. It took me a long time, perhaps an hour, maybe more, but my family and the man who ran the place waited without comment. He had grown to understand the importance of grieving process though many years of close association with it and even though it was late at night, he had stayed open waiting for my plane to arrive.

I was devastated but comforted by the nearness of the strong females in my family. I too share their inner strength and sheer determination to live life with joy when possible, and grim acceptance when the former is not an option. When I had seen as much of my brother as I could cope with, my grandmother photographed his body. Yes, we photograph our dead in my family. Births are celebrated with photographs and we believe that a family member's passing from this world should be shown the same devotion. For me, these photographs have helped me accept the fact that my brother really is dead, that he actually will never again sling his arm round my neck and laughingly pull me close so he can tickle me as I squirm away. He did not have Asperger's syndrome and loved physical contact as much as our mom does. I am thankful she has had the pleasure of one affectionate child who easily gave her what I can not.

We all piled into 2 cars and left the funeral home, I felt sick with tiredness and sodden with unshed grief. When we got back to my aunt's we grieved in a fashion I could join in with. We laughed at happy memories of times we had shared together, looked through hundreds of pictures, drank champagne and played scrabble to relax and soothe our addled brains. I am blessed with a weird but wonderful family. My mom and aunt told a strange story that night.

Mom had phoned her to break the devastating news and then after they said good bye to each other, they both simultaneously tried to phone the same one of my aunts who lived in Eastern Canada. None of them have conference calling and yet they suddenly were all connected and able to speak to each other, at the same time! It wasn't until they ended the call that the significance of what had just happened dawned on them...did my brother somehow have a hand in connecting the phone lines? We'll never know.

The next day, 2 car loads of us drove to the spot where he was killed. The burgundy stain on the yellow lines was shockingly large; I tried to tell myself it didn't matter...Jia didn't need that blood anymore. That stain's portrayal of violent death was in complete contrast with the luxuriant, copiously lush foliage that grew along the sides of the highway. The scent of Cedar wood that emanated from the sawmills always accompanies this memory as if trying to purify the impact of the image. I remember feeling saddened to note that there was a restaurant with a deck, facing the expanse of highway. Anyone who had been innocently sat there would have been unfortunate enough to observe the moment the huge hay truck hit and killed my brother while he was working as a surveyor on that section of road. I say unfortunate for them as that memory will surely disturb them forever as it will my brother's colleague who was working with him that day. I also can accept that the truck driver will be scarred for life. It all seems such a waste; it will never bring my brother back so why should they have to be punished by their memories of a man they did not share a life with?

My mom and I travelled back to my mother's once we had collected Jia's ashes. My aunt, grandmother and cousins arrived the next day and we spent the next morning putting together a memorial album, bringing it to life with our laughter, blessing it with our tears. We put the album on the top table with vases of Dahlia's which were lavishly , abundantly in season along with some other important items for family and friends to look at and hold if they wished. It seemed wrong that we used cut flowers. I now wish that we had bought flowering plants in pots and then put them in the ground to continue to grow after the ceremony. It somehow seems wrong to have killed a plant so that we could honour a loved one who had died…

My cousins and I went through his belongings that evening. Jia had turned 21 that year. I had of course remembered it was a significant birthday for him but I had remembered too late to send a card in time for his birthday and for some reason never bothered to send a belated birthday wish. I have always been terrible at remembering dates of special events, including ones that happen yearly and even if they are written on the calendar. To my shame I saw he had kept every birthday card he got for that birthday, there was a figurative black hole where mine should have been. In its place was every single letter I had ever written him. I began to cry when I saw that…my brother had just shown me how very much he loved me. I wish that I had taken the time to tell him how very much I loved him, one last time before he had been killed. I still forget to send birthday cards sometimes but I make a point as often as possible, to tell everyone I love that I love them. Just in case...

The next day my father phoned. This was a shock in itself as he shares my abhorrence of phones. He told me he was coming to get me and to take me to his place for a couple of days. This was a second shock as my father is more than a bit of a recluse and my mother lived a good 8 hours round trip from his home.

When I protested that my mother needed me, he responded with 'You've still got two brothers who are very much alive and wanting to see you!'.

I stopped protesting, he was right. I spent a few restorative days wandering on my dad's land, breathing in some peace and made sure to tell my brothers that I loved them. They are energetic, deep thinkers and full of life. I also tell Jia I love him; to me he is still vibrant but shimmering with life elsewhere. Someday I shall post that birthday card to him and then perhaps I can move on from this silent grief.

A golden feather

I gave my love a golden feather
A gift of the heart to forever treasure
A golden feather – a rare sight to behold
From an angel's wing it came, of the purest gold

It floated softly between us and stayed
In the cocoon of our loving it gently swayed
Its golden glow filled us with such wondrous delight
As we made our promises in the still of the night

My love used the feather to paint himself bold
He smoothed his raw edges with the feather's gold
All the stories he embroidered as he told
In a false light he cast himself in a new mould

Then the days of hate came with words of scorn
Furniture flying with curses, feelings all torn
The feather dropped down heavy as a rock
And stayed there while he threatened and mocked

Words that scorched one side so charcoal black
Curled and charred the feather gave no light back
He bent and picked it up while I stood so still
Into my heart's blood he dipped the quill

And attempted to write the words, 'I'm sorry'
Each letter a painful jab into my hearts story
The cost of those words a cold numb dread
For I had to leave my heart and follow my head

Under his boots was a dust of gold
'Oh rich are we', he seized it with glee
I could not smile with a mouth so cold
I wanted only my feather of gold.

The above poem was written by my mom about her relationship with Dick.

Dot's Café

Mom, Jia and I had to travel to the 'Main Land' in order to attend our twice monthly appointments with Brenda. This was a major expedition including a drive of several hours and a 2 ½ hour ferry trip. On the way home, all of us emotionally wrung out and sick at heart, mom would stop for gas. At the far end of the station, on the same bit of land, was Dot's Café. The huge lemon meringue pie sign atop of the caravan and was visible from a long distance in either direction on the highway.

Dot's cafe was housed in a large silver caravan with extra seating in a forest green wooden conservatory built on the front. Inside the silver bullet shaped trailer were several booths which butted up against the conservatory windows, a space to walk and then bars tools in front of a counter which ensured front seat views of the cook frying up your meal on either the grill or the deep fryer. Other than a sandwich, your choice for main course consisted of fried food or fried food but the dessert was bright yellow sunshine. Dot's cafe served the best lemon meringue pie anywhere, even better than my mom's!

Looking back now I suspect that mom may also have needed to stop at Dot's to feed her munchies. She loved to drive but most especially after she had smoked a spliff and cranked the music and I suspect that high would have been most welcome after a harrowing visit to see Brenda and then having to ignore her own pain so she could help us deal with ours. My brother and I loved the smell of dope and the sound of her music so everyone was happier by the time we reached Dot's... though I always thought she drove a bit too fast. I used to really piss her off by craning my body over to the left so I could watch the speedometer and comment in outraged tones when she tipped over the upper speed limit. I wish I could tell you I outgrew that habit but it wouldn't be right to lie to someone who was kind enough to buy this book!

Rice cakes and apple juice

I used to suffer from excruciating stomach pains when we lived with Dick. Many mornings I would lie on the couch moaning with the waves of pain in my stomach. They only ever occurred in the mornings and soon passed but while I had them I thought I would die. They must have worried mum too as one morning she phoned the doctor so he could listen to me as I cried out. I got admitted to hospital for a series of tests, most of them unpleasant and none that revealed anything amiss. Someone mentioned the possibility of an ulcer to mom and she put me on a diet of bland food and buttermilk. Bleauuugh. Once we escaped from Dick the pains eased and then vanished completely. This was my first and only experience of psychosomatic pain, which some would describe as imagined pain. Well I can tell you that, imagined it may have been but my brain is connected to my body and that pain felt very real indeed.

I have written of my fear of what Dick would do when he found out I had told others of his calculating madness. Even though we had moved from the Island to the larger Island, it was only a 15 minute ferry ride and I would occasionally see him driving the streets. Mom assured me that he did not know where we lived but I was aware that he sure as hell knew where I went to school and I would go through elaborate routes home to ensure he was not able to follow me. My imagination got the better of me however and no matter how elaborate and lengthy the route home became, I was convinced he had outmanoeuvred me and now knew where we lived.

A fertile imagination can be a dangerous thing if left to wander on its own and mine soon convinced me that Dick must be poisoning my food. He knew how much I loved to eat so what better way to get at me without anyone noticing? Eventually all I could bring myself to eat with out shrivelling up with fear was rice cakes and apple juice. I developed a mild phobia about food poisoning that I battle with to this day. I do not remember introducing other foods onto my safe list but I am quite robust (some would say overweight but I think selective hearing is a wonderful thing and utilise it frequently in these instances) and I now eat a widely varied diet.

Now that I am an adult and living on a different continent than Dick, my worries over food poisoning have morphed into a reluctance to eat any meat with even an infinitesimal possibility of being undercooked or using any product that is out of date. I can look at the situation logically and recognise the ridiculousness of these fears but that little girl inside of me knows otherwise and is still convinced that Dick will win this battle and if I let down my guard, food will make me very ill. Logic is all very well but that scared little girl is inside me and therefore her fears hold more weight than the sheer reasonableness of logic.

Buddy

By the time I was 15, I was becoming increasingly popular with my peers. However, inside I was still struggling with the knowledge that I was in no way, shape or form the same as them. My mind worked differently, I saw things as flavours and smells and tasted things with a visual aspect in addition to the experience of the flavour. On the plus side, my normal world resembled the Aurora Borealis, I frequently had to suppress the urge to exclaim 'wow' at a sensation or flavour and I knew of no one else who experienced this. On the negative side, lights were too bright, smells were often overpowering, sounds were too loud and I never ever got 'the joke'!

For some reason no one noticed or commented on what I thought was my glaring weirdness any longer and I got invited to more and more trendy teenage gatherings and began to climb the social ladder of popularity. One day Buddy came into my life and I immediately welcomed him into my world. I cannot begin to describe the sensation of his warm feathers brushing against my chin and neck. It was exquisitely comforting and in my mind, set off images of wispy, gossamer webs that climbed over each other, changing shapes much in the way that a tangible Mandela will. It is incredibly difficult to explain how sensations affect me, how they appear in my mind as images and scents. I now know that this is not unusual for people with Asperger's but at this point in history Asperger's had not even gained classification as a 'disability', as far as the medical world was concerned Asperger's did not exist.

I thought there was nothing unusual in the fact that I walked around with a wild bird named Buddy on my shoulder. What is even more remarkable is neither did any of the people in my social circle, or maybe they were just used to my unique behaviours and refrained from comment.... Luckily this happened during the summer school break as I am certain my teachers would have had plenty of negative things to say about a bird attending school.

I am not sure why Buddy came into my life but for the few weeks he lived with me before he inexplicably died I treasured his company and he seemed comfortable in mine

Candy striper

During my short time spent in hospital with stomach pains, I spotted girls my age who wore the sweetest pink and white stripped uniforms. I coveted one of those uniforms and asked what kind of a nurse they were. To my delight I was told that they were volunteers. The thought of those uniforms played on my mind for a few years and eventually I made my way to the hospital reception and collected an application form. Unlike a lot of people, I enjoyed the hospital environment.

Designed and decorated to sooth and heal sick people, the colours were subdued and noises were stifled. It reduced the distractions of normal life for me and I was able to relax for hours at a time without having to process all the sensory input that usually led to overload and the subsequent apparent lack of focus. I was focussed all right but inwardly, on the business of my mind as it tried to suitably process all the stuff that had gone in and was now revolving round without alighting at the correct stop. The lack of sensory adaptation may have unconsciously been deliberate as the sensations were more intriguing and enjoyable to the extreme rather than distressing and unwelcome.

During my time as a candy stripper I ran errands, served food and made beds. Occasionally I was allowed to help out on what used to be referred to as the 'geriatric' ward. While there the staff would encourage me to sit with the elderly patients during meal times in the communal dining room. I would sometimes help feed those who could not do it themselves or sit with those who would quickly go vacant and forget to eat unless someone gave them a regular nudge of encouragement. I tried not to look as horrified as I felt when I spotted the more able bodied, though not necessarily able minded, residents taking out their dentures and licking them clean. I always felt a great sense of pride as I walked to and from a shift in the hospital. I wanted people to stop me in the street and exclaim over my crisp uniform, I wanted to be able to shout out how much I enjoyed being a volunteer, how special this selfless giving of my time was.

However, like most teenagers, there was also a 'Mr Hyde' side to my personality, an alter ego which wanted to rebel, to be as disagreeable as possible. The crowd that I was hanging out with had started to experiment with hash. I had never tired hash before but knew from an experience at my dad's that cannabis was not my drug of choice. I still spent the occasional weekend with my dad. He had moved back to the Island and was living with the woman who was to become my stepmother when I was 16. She did her best to tolerate my stays with them but as a step mother myself I can imagine the disruption that my visits caused. I clung to every nuance my father uttered and as he was a very early riser, I would get up at 4.30am with him and stay up until I was dropping with tiredness.

Since my first cigarette at the age of 12 I had indulged on occasion, addicted but able to go long periods without nicotine due to lack of funds. My father smoked too and one evening he must have noticed the lust in my eyes as I watched his hand take yet another menthol cigarette from the pack, tap it and then place it in his mouth before lighting it.
'You want one? They're menthol, you won't like them!' he said.
Determined that if my dad smoked them then they were the brand for me, I said 'oh yes please!' and smoked it from tip to filter luxuriating in the sensation of the menthol

cooling my throat. From that moment on till I quit at the age of 32 I smoked nothing but menthol cigarettes.

Later that same evening a few neighbours came round. I sat at the table with them, of course. My dad rolled a fat joint and I avidly watched every movement his fingers made. How clever, I thought, to be able to take scraps of plant, a flimsy bit of paper and roll it between 4 fingers and 2 thumbs to make a near perfect cylinder of it all. The joint was light and passed round amongst the adults till it was a tiny too hot roach. I inhaled deeply with each breath; I had always loved the smell of dope and the peace it brought with it. I wasn't aware of being mildly stoned myself though I suppose I must have been. This evening, when they sparked up another joint, my dad offered me a toke with a grin on his face. I think now that he must have been teasing me, not expecting me to accept as I had never shown an interest in experimenting with drugs. I surprised us all by taking it and filling my lungs with its sweet scent. With alarming rapidity I was very stoned and I hated it! My head buzzed, I could not feel my skin and my ears rang. I stood up to make my way up stairs to bed and fainted half way up. I must have acted oddly enough to concern my dad as he was behind me and caught me before I could fall. I slept it off and that was the last time I ever smoked cannabis.

My friends knew of this story and reassured me that the 'stone' from hash was nothing like that of cannabis. Somewhat reluctantly I agreed to join in with the hot knifing session. I took two knives and holding one in each hand I heated the tips between the electric elements on the stove. Once they were glowing red I pinched a tiny roll of hash between them and inhaled the smoke. Whammo! Exactly the same sensation as before at my dads but minus the ear ringing which I had come to know meant a faint wasn't far off. Pissed off at what I perceived to be my friends deceit I stomped across the road to the apartment I lived in with mom and Jia. I then endured a lecture from her while she rubbed my arms firmly. She kept this up for ages so that I could feel the sensation and in order to prevent me freaking out and hitting my arms to produce the same effect. There ended my experimentation with all inhale-able drugs except for nicotine which was to remain my dangerous, money burning, health destroying love for many more years.

Hot boxing

That winter my mom was out of a job for the first time in years. She had to go on welfare and still she struggled to make ends meet. By Christmas things were pretty desperate and we were given a welfare food box. These boxes were made up from donations given to the food bank and at this time of the year were quite generously filled. Although my mother hated having to accept welfare donations, I thought it a wondrous experience to be given several large boxes of food for free. They included Christmas meal basics like a turkey, vegetables and stuffing mix and exciting, usually forbidden, treats like boxed macaroni with little packets of cheese power which turned into sauce when mixed with milk and butter. The boxes also had presents for me and my brother. I remember one of them was a candle holder in the shape of a lotus flower. The petals were made of mother of pearl and framed in gold coloured metal. I loved that gift and sat for many hours angling it so the light would catch and bounce off the leaves made of that fragile shell. I kept it on a shelf next to the record player and could see it vibrate when music poured out of the nearby speakers.

I think having a sneaky party while your parent is away is some modern form of a rite of passage. I never planned mine as such; it was supposed to be just a couple of friends over, but those friends told a few friends, who told a few friends and so on. Within a few hours the house was full! I was beside myself with joy about my total coolness at having such a rocking party and despair at having to cope with this invasion of people in my home. I felt tainted by their noise and the strangeness of their faces and body odour.

They invaded every corner of my house and left me feeling as if my most delicate orifices had been roughly probed by unwelcome fingers. The tiny box room where the toilet and shower were was immediately appropriated by the 'stoners'. They crammed several people in there, shut the window and door and proceeded to 'hotbox' the room. There must have been a gap under the door as soon the house was full of the smell of 'skunk weed', which back in those days was a very inexpensive and skunky smelling type of cannabis.

Eventually the neighbour came to the front door to complain about the noise. Instantly the noise from the rest of the partiers diminished, enough to appease the woman from next door. I wouldn't let her past the front door as I didn't want her to see that the house was full of teenagers though I now suspect that she may have seen the steady stream of bodies as they had arrived over the past hour. I had a beer and someone put on ZZ Top's Sharp Dressed Man on the record player. Instantly, I was lost in the feel of the music. I have always loved the way music feels in my body and if the music is loud enough it shuts out everything else around me, a form of sensory overload I guess. Anyone who didn't know me that evening, which was many people, would have thought my drink had been spiked with drugs, I was gone! I remember nothing else between that first guitar rift and the loud pounding on the door which announced the Police's presence and urgent desire to be let in. That snapped me out of my music trip very quickly. I have no idea how I instinctively knew it was the Police but I hustled to the door feeling guilty and scared.

Once all the people in the house had been herded out by the unexpectedly pleasant police, I was left on my own to clear the debris, relieved they were gone and hoping naively that I could keep mom from finding out how many people had actually been in the house. I didn't think the Police would bother coming back to talk to her and I was certain the neighbour didn't know the true numbers. I can't understand why I didn't consider the fact that she had a front window and was quite capable of watching the streams of people vacate. Which she had! Man, was I in trouble when my mom got back the next day.

By the time I had collected all the beer bottles, our large kitchen table was covered in rows of stubbies which touched each other from every angle except top and bottom. I gloated over the fact that my coolness quotient was going to be sky high among my peers. Maybe having to cope with the house full of people had been worth it after all. I placed the bottles in a big rubbish sack and put them out the back door. I had plans to take them to the recycling dept and collect the refund, 5 cents per bottle would add up to a decent amount in total.

While cleaning I found my lotus flower candle holder under the couch. The leaves were bent and one of them was missing its mother of pearl filler. I cried as I placed it in the garbage, it was too beautiful to be discarded and I realised then that every action has a consequence, something gained often means something lost. That gift from a kind stranger had been worth far more to me than gaining credibility with a bunch of strangers who happened to be in my age group. The truth of the matter was that I did not need their approval and company to enjoy myself but I had lost an important aspect of my ability to calm myself and enter into my own world when that mother of pearl Mandela got damaged. To this day, house parties make me anxious and I have to restrain myself from stepping rudely in front of guests if they seem to be getting too close to an object I particularly cherish.

I thought that I did a good job of clearing up the mess but I missed a bottle under mom's bed which she found. Also there was a long, wide blue streak which swept all along the white wall which ran the length of the stairs. I could not scrub that mark off no matter what cleaning product I tried and gave up knowing that I had some explaining to do.

Absolutely incapable of lying, (exaggerations, half-truths and strategic omissions are as close as I can get), I had no option but to tell her the truth. I am not sure what she was more angry about, the bottle under her bed, which meant someone had been in her room, the damaged wall, which needed a coat of paint to repair or that I hadn't asked her permission to have the party. She was so broke that she hadn't been able to afford to buy us Christmas presents that year and the thought of having to spend money on house repairs must have made her despair. Luckily I had a part time job and she made me pay for the paint and supervised me carefully while I covered the wall. I think she must have been extremely brave or very angry to let me do the painting as I was still painfully clumsy and likely to get more on the floor and on myself than actually on the wall!

I found appearance of the paint left by each brush stroke absolutely mesmerising and it took me far longer to put one coat on than one might expect. I had to stop and admire each feathery, slightly iridescent streak before I applied the next and made sure that the next stroke followed the last in a precisely parallel path, however the final paint job was done to perfection if I do say so myself. I learnt that house parties were more fun in someone else's and I could never paint interiors for a living; I would be exhausted by the time I had finished one room, let alone a whole house!

On fire

My dad no longer worked in the music store but was now employed as a fisherman. He worked with his girlfriend's brother on his boat, fishing and acting as engineer when needed. The fishing season begins in February, in the most horrid weather to be found in our area of the world so that they could make the most of the herring season and then fish throughout the year, enjoying nicer weather as the seasons progressed. The fishing season ran about 6 months of the year, a few more spent on boat maintenance etc and then dad was free to work his land. At first he could only afford to buy 7 acres but he now owns 15 acres in one of the most remote and beautiful spots on the Island. Although he, my stepmother and a few hardy others have lived out there since the late 70's, it has taken until 2008 for there to be serious attempts to get electricity from the main Island out to the inhabitants of that secluded Bay.

Back then when my dad and his soon to be wife, Bonnie first lived there, they had 7 acres of wooded land and kerosene lamps. Running water at the turn of a tap and a generator to run appliances was a distant dream. At first Dad lived in what later got used as the sauna, which should give you some idea of how small the building was. Soon after Bonnie joined his life he built a somewhat larger log cabin and dug out a large pond around the sauna. Nowadays the pond is sadly dry and overgrown with grass and small trees but back then the pond was filled deep enough for me to paddle around in it floating in a child sized kayak. The winters were cold enough to have a decent snowfall on occasion and I can remember seeing stoned and very hot adults (my dad, his best friend or the neighbours usually) leaping from the sauna's steps into the pond or snow banks before moving at speed back into the warmth of the sauna. I watched them and laughed from the comfort of the hot little room which struggled to hold more than 6 adults and which my dad had once thought large enough to call home.

The spring after my house party my dad was clearing more of his land, determined to get enough space for a garden. The trees which he deemed large enough were kept for later building use. He peeled the bark off by hand using an instrument that looked like a large chisel head mounted on a shovel pole with a handle at the opposite end. He made it look easy as the bark separated like butter from the logs but when I tried I could barely lift the tool let alone part the bark from its home. The trimmings such as branches and root stock were thrown on a pile to be burnt later. The piles grew over the year at an impressive rate and I begged dad not to light them unless it was a weekend that I was staying with him. That fall on one of my weekend visits he decided to light the largest pile near the pond.

We had been experiencing wet weather off and on during the summer, not unusual for the Island but eventually we got to this point in the year and had enjoyed a few weeks of cool but dry weather.

Eagerly I watched dad move around the pile, poking it and stuffing newspapers into crevices. He continued doing this for what I finally decided was an unreasonable amount of time.

'Whatcha doin dad?' I shifted from foot to foot as I spoke, trying to fidget away my impatience.

He sighed in exasperation. 'The bonfire pile must have been thoroughly saturated. I tried to light it on the other side but it didn't catch.' He came around to the side I could see and demonstrated.

I could see the match flare towards the newspaper which flamed towards the middle of the bottom of the huge pile and then blink out.

'I should have kicked it apart to dry out when the dry weather stuck.' Dad stood up and placed his hands on his hips, bend backwards to unkink his spine.

'I'm never going to get to see a bonfire!' I said petulantly, like a child half my age.

Bonnie said 'There will be other bonfires.'

'I waited all year for this one!'

We both fell silent as my dad walked away from us.

'Len?' Bonnie followed him as he moved in the direction of the wood shed.

I walked around the pile of damp wood debris a couple of times, stopping on the side facing the pond. I kicked at a large stone trying to dislodge it, sulking.

'Okay let's see what luck we have with this. If it doesn't work then I am all out of ideas.' Dad hefted a container in the air; Bonnie followed him carrying a small ladder. He climbed the ladder while Bonnie steadied it.

'Stand back.' He ordered.

I moved away until I had to stop or else fall into the pond. 'Far enough dad?'

'He peered over the top of the pile to gauge my distance and nodded his head. Dad poured the fluid onto the top of the pile and followed it with a match. Nothing happened and I watched disappointed as he began to climb down the ladder.

'WHUOOOMF!' bellowed the fire as it blew out of the bottom of one side of the pile and wrapped itself around my ankles.

I shrieked, more from fright than pain. As an adult I now know that I do not interpret pain signals the same as a neurotypical person might but at the time I registered very little pain so I did not react other than to cry out. I stood mesmerised by the sight of the fire which had receded back into the pile and the flames were shooting from the top as they should.

'Move away!' dad shouted as he leapt to the ground and ran towards me. I was dimly aware of air pushing against me as dad rushed towards me. The next thing I knew he had picked me up and set me feet first into the pond!

'Dad!' I scolded, confused and wondering if I should be amused. Was this a joke? I never 'get' jokes in that instinctive, almost instantaneous fashion that others do.

'The fire was wrapped around your ankles, your trousers were smouldering! I had to put them out fast. Get out of the pond and lets have a look at you.'

Other than some redness around my ankles I appeared to have escaped unscathed. Dad declared that I was luckier than I had any right to be and I was allowed to watch the bonfire, from a safe distance. I watched fascinated by the play of the flame, the myriad of colours which leapt around the burning wood as it changed from sap filled new growth to wizened disintegrating logs, until it was no more than flickering embers and dad doused the remaining charcoal with shovelful's of dirt.

I went home the next day with a few blisters on my red ankles. To say my mom was not happy would be an understatement and I listened with embarrassment as she told my father by phone exactly what she thought of his child care skills. I felt fine but she knew me too well. She then recounted a story of when I was a child of about 4 and had fallen into a pail full of my youngest cousin's nappies. They were soaking in boiling water, safely placed in the middle of the bathtub or so mom thought. Apparently she found me after I had fallen into the pail while trying to stir the contents! I wouldn't let her look at my arm even though she knew I must be burnt and sore and she said I even laid on my arm to stop her looking at it. Yes I was and still am very stubborn! She said I never complained about that burn and it made so little impact on me that I don't even remember the incident.

By the following day the blisters on my ankle were very large about the size of the base of a cupcake. She made a doctor's appointment for me, ignoring my protests that I had a curling match that evening. I was the junior skip for the city, very proud of my position on the team and reluctant to miss a game for an injury that wasn't even causing me any pain. However mom insisted I go promising that I could go to the match after if the doctor gave his approval. He didn't! I had 3rd degree burns in places on each ankle and had to have the dead skin cut away during several visits. I had huge bandages on each ankle but after my check up at the end of the week I just smiled when mom asked me if I was allowed to play. By the end of the game there were two large blood stains on each bright white bandage and that was the end of my curling for that season! I have a few tiny brown scars on my ankle to this day, hardly seems a fitting mark for all the hassle it caused.

Porno Noise Pollution

Gritting my teeth didn't help, it just made them hurt. I sighed and turned loudly over in bed, then clamped my pillow over my head in an attempt to drown out the noise. There were always men in my mom's life. In fact not long after we escaped the curmudgeon a man named Maurice appeared on the scene. He was absolutely lovely, a big bearded gentle bear of a man. Mom seemed to enjoy his company, too much at this time of night in my opinion! I rolled back over, picked up a text book that I had been reading before I went to sleep and threw it hard against the wall.

Sudden silence drifted across to me. I grinned with satisfaction, peace at last.

'Denyse? What was that?' Mom's voice sounded puzzled but of course she knew.

'Me! I hit the wall with a book!'

'Why?'

''Cos I want to sleep and I can't with all that noise!'

Blessed silence descended. Welcome sweet sleep.

The next morning I had got a telling off from mom for my 'rude' behaviour and I retaliated that having noisy sex which kept others in the house from sleeping was just as inexcusable! I felt vindicated when one of our neighbours called round to tease mom about the porno movie they could hear during the night, seems mom had forgotten that her windows were open and at last she realised that perhaps I was justified in saying she made too much noise during sex. I am often singularly focussed on achieving my intended goal, in this case a good night's sleep, that I am often accused of being cold or harsh. I do not intend to be unkind or to make anyone feel bad about themselves in these instances but I can see that I used to put my needs before other people. I am more aware of the inappropriateness of this kind of behaviour now and put a lot of effort into trying to meet people's expectations of me on a more frequent basis, although until in my mid 30's I was still being told by 'significant' others that I was rude, inaccessible or frigid. I now console myself with the notion that their inaccurate perception and interpretation of my behaviour was not always entirely my fault.

My hearing is undeniably more acute than other people's though not necessarily in a useful way. If there is any background noise then I find this very distracting and can not concentrate on what I am suppose to. However, in the quiet of the middle of the night, it seems I can hear everything and amplified a hundred times. We call it the 'bionic ear syndrome' and several women in our family suffer from it so I suspect it is more of a genetic thing rather than an autistic trait. Certainly it is one I would be happy to un-inherit!

How not to gas a cat

That year I began my second to last year of school and like most of my peers, was growing increasingly bored with the daily drudge of attending classes. History class was always first thing and our teacher was going through his Nazi phase. No I am not referring to his behaviour but the era he was teaching us about. Each history class we were bombarded with movies and still pictures of the atrocities that the victims had endured until their very souls had no option but to leave in despair. I sat at the front table a little to the right of the movie screen because there were never any other seats left when I arrived at the last possible second before the start of class bell sounded.

One day I arrived a few minutes early and was occupying myself with watching the flecks of spit gather in the corner of my teacher's mouth as he spoke energetically to another student.

'Mind if I sit here?' a girl's voice said in a tone that expected only agreement.

'Um yah no problem... cool!' I said as I looked round and realised that it was one of the most popular girls in the school. What the hell was she doing sitting with me I wondered. Barbie normally sat at the very rear of the class, chewing gum, flicking her blonde hair and looking incredibly perfect in a rebel rather than sorority girl kind of way.

Embarrassed at my geeky reaction, knowing I would never be as aloof and desperately attractive as Barbie, I stared at the table hoping she would speak again. I groaned involuntarily as the dimming of the lights announced yet another shocking film.

Barbie said 'C'mon!' and stood up.

Flustered, not wanting to lose her attention, I followed suit.

'Mr A?' He turned to look in our direction.

'I feel pretty sick, woman's troubles...' her voice dropped to a confidential whisper on the word woman and he nodded his permission as we made our escape.

'Where we going?' I said once we got in the hallway wondering how much trouble we were going to get into because Barbie had lied. I was a tragic liar and got caught out every time; I assumed this was the same for everyone.

'Dunno...coffee?'

'Okay...' I said trying not to sound as scared as I felt. 'What if we get caught?'

'Don't be such a loser, 'corse we won't get caught! I told him I am on the rag and he ain't coming in the girl's toilet is he?'

'Loser! Hah! That's funny!' I said without actually laughing and while hoping all the same that she was joking. I followed her out the back door of the school, across the field and over to the café on the other side of the road. I drank cinnamon tea, Barbie had coffee and a friendship was born that would span boyfriends, shared accommodation, first orgasms and subsequent lack of, marriages, leaving our hometowns to work in other Provinces, childbirth and divorces over the next 22 years was formed.

Barbie lived in a town which was over 50 miles away from where we went to high school. I walked to school in ten minutes and she was bussed in each day, a trip of over an hour both ways. I began to spend time at Barbie's house during the week, this obviously meant an overnight stay but the disruption to my routine was worth the opportunity to spend time in Barbie's orbit. I felt almost normal around her and the rest of our peers in Sayward did not dare question the acceptability of one of Barbie's inner circle.

It was during these visits that I first realised that I had issues with vomit. I spent the occasional weekend at Barbie's and on those occasions we would go to parties where people would drink too much and sometimes puke. Never either of us luckily! I would be trying very hard to enjoy myself without the aid of alcohol which I wasn't comfortable drinking yet and then someone would suddenly vomit. No effort to get to a toilet mind you! On more than one occasion I had the misfortune to be unable to look away in time and would watch as a person simply opened their mouth and spewed the contents of their stomach out onto wherever they sat or lay. Disgusting! I can not describe the repulsion I felt at the sight, sound and smell of their effluence. Irrationally, I admit, I would be seized with the desire to punch them hard enough to penetrate through their alcohol haze and hurt them.

I can remember experiencing the same surge of anger once when I was about 5 and ended up chasing a girl who had been teasing me, down the street. With a skipping rope slung over my shoulders, knowing I would beat her with it if I caught up. The urge to hurt her was a physical force, a red fog that blurred my reason. My mother came out and caught me; boy was I in trouble for my behaviour, which I was unable to explain to her satisfaction. It was many years before I got my temper completely under control and many more before I was able to stop blurting out my disgust at people's behaviour if they offended me. By the time I began my midwifery training, it was still a sufficient challenge for me and one which I had to overcome before I was able to compete my training and register as a midwife.

I returned home from a weekend away at Barbie's to find that my cat Kitty-Bear had gone missing. I was devastated as he was my comfort during the long night when my over active mind and hyper sensitive hearing would keep me awake. I would stroke his fur as he lay beside me, purring. Years later I was lucky enough to welcome a cat with a very similar personality into my life, his name is Foxy and he too sleeps beside me at night, keeping the things that 'go creak in the night' at bay. I always sleep better if he is stretched out beside me.

I moped around for a week, heart sick and longing to hear Kitty-Bear meow at the door. He never came and I began to walk the streets of our neighbourhood calling for him and when eventually I worked up the nerve to look in ditches for his body. What other reason could there be for his failure to come home? Someone suggested I look in the animal impound and I went immediately there after school that day. To my great joy and his, Kitty-Bear was there! The person at the desk said a woman had turned him in as a homeless stray over a week ago and admonished me for not having a collar and tag on him. I paid for one immediately and walked the mile home with him held close. His hind legs rested on my forearm and his front paws held onto my shoulder, his purrs roaring in my ears and whiskers tickling my skin.

There was no need to worry about his escaping, Kitty-Bear knew where he belonged and I knew that if I put him down he would follow me home. When Kitty-Bear and I arrived home, mom's look of shock was not the mirror of my smile that I had expected but I was too caught up in my joy to question her. Many years later after numerous glasses of champagne and some second hand cannabis smoke had loosened her tongue she confessed. She had put Kitty-Bear in a burlap potato sack and held him in the fumes from her car's exhaust, when this failed to kill him she had taken him to the pound claiming he was a stray! When I asked why she had done this she simply said she was too poor to be able to afford to feed him. I wonder why I was not expected to pay for his food; I did work and had done so for years. I can't remember but expect like most teenagers I spent all of my meagre pay on myself, probably on the cigarettes that my mother did not know I smoked.

Wedding weeping

This is my most embarrassing memory for I humiliated myself to such an extent that it is still mentioned now, 24 years after the event.

My dad and Bonnie decided to get married and I was invited, something which I am sure Bonnie still regrets. My father's mother and father were there and although I do not remember meeting them as a young child, I bonded with them instantly. My Grammie Kirkby is a very affectionate woman but not in the way that normally makes my skin crawl. When she wraps me in her arms, I feel as if all the microscopic fissures on my body (that are usually held open by the static of life's stress), give a sigh of relief as they close.

To my dismay, I cried through the entire wedding ceremony, my sobs growing louder and louder until my grandparents had to remove me from the church and take me to a nearby restaurant where they plied themselves and me with Pina Colada's and sympathy until I had calmed down. I now know that I am incapable of attending weddings or funerals but at the time of this wedding, I was completely unprepared for the effect it would have on me and thought my reaction was due to something other than the circumstance. I know that I have mentioned, many times, in this memoir that I have heightened senses of touch, taste, scents, sight and sound and I am very attuned to lights, noises, textures and smells. It doesn't take much for me to go into sensory overload which normally involves me going off into 'my own world' for a while until I can adapt to these overwhelming sensations and return the participate in whatever I was currently involved in. However, for some reason when I am at a wedding or funeral, this sensory overload manifest itself as hysterical weeping. My father and Bonnie's wedding was my first experience of this reaction, how I wish I knew then what I do now, that I can not attend these events. At least then everyone would have understood that, truly, I was not unhappy they were getting married, I was just overwhelmed by the whole experience. By the time my best friend's father died, I understood enough about myself to know that I could not support her by attending is funeral as my sorrow for her would manifest itself as hysterical grief and I would be of no use to her. Elaine did not question me when I declined to attend the funeral and I know that I am very lucky to still have her as a very dear friend as our friendship weathered this situation which occurred long before I was diagnosed!

A place of my own

I struggled in my final year of school. There were only two courses I enjoyed, biology and English literature, the rest were a dull chore beyond endurance which I avoided as often as possible. I scraped through my final exams, ending my schooling with an average pass as my overall mark and no qualifications in math as I had stopped taking math classes when I was 14. Back then you had to have a credit in a language or maths and so I cheated by taking French class which was ridiculously easy due to having spoken French for so many years as a young child. I have a MENSA confirmed IQ of 138 which I have been told puts me in the top 6% of the population and by this point I had learnt to put it to good use by manipulating situations to my advantage in order to make my life as pleasant as possible! By the time I had graduated I was desperate to move out on my own.

Things were intolerable at home, in my opinion and my mom did not seem devastated to hear I was planning to move out. At first I lived with my step mom's sister, Aunty Joan. I thought she was a wonderful woman, she was incredibly tolerant of me, and made me feel loved even when I was going through a phase of being most unlovable. I had a room of my own in her ground floor family room and would have stayed there inevitably if my behaviour had not made me feel it necessary for me to leave. Aunty Joan's daughter Dana was really sweet and came close to feeling like my kid sister. I enjoyed her company and she was so goofy and light hearted about life in general that she never failed to make me laugh. There was a man she had a crush on named Eric, I am certain he was too old for her and am not sure if they were dating or not. However for reasons that are unclear to me, I too became infatuated with him. We struck up a friend ship that soon became more and I knew that I had to move out into a place of my own.

A ground floor, one bedroom apartment, across from mom's place became available. Mom vouched for me with the landlord and I moved in. I was working full time serving behind the concessions counter at the bingo hall and could afford to pay the rent. What I had not considered was how little I would have left over after paying the rest of the bills! The end of that first month living in that lovely little apartment came as quite a shock when I realised the amount of money I had left to buy food with and I realised that I would have to get someone to share the place and bills with me if I was going to continue living there. I knew that there was only one person I could tolerate living with and so I asked Barbie if she would like to move in. She agreed to join me there at the end of the month. Meanwhile Eric and my relationship had progressed to something more than platonic. I had no idea if he was still involved with Dana and I never asked her preferring to not know the answer. This was not the first time I would follow instinct when it came to embarking on a relationship with a man and every time, bar one, I would come to regret my actions. One day, shortly after I had moved in, he was visiting and the doorbell rang announcing an unexpected visit from Dana.

To my shame, I remember that Eric and I were listening to Robert Palmer's Addicted to Love and the only comment she made was 'Eric I thought that was our song?' Although my behaviour was never questioned by my family, I am sure that I hurt Dana and wish I had apologised at the time. If only she had come just a few short weeks later when the relationship had fizzled out into an amicable friendship...

I have never been any good with apologising but Dana, I am sorry, and to this day I do not understand why I behaved the way I did.

Nomad

Barbie and I shared that lovely little one bedroom apartment for the better part of a year. I had the bedroom and paid slightly more of the rent and she made the living room her own space. She began to socialise more and more at our place and the situation began to stress me out enough that I began to look at moving out. One of the girls I had known in high school told me that she had heard that the Banff Springs Hotel was hiring and if you could afford to travel out there then they paid for your food and accommodation. I had a look at the advert in the paper, decided that I could afford the train fare and Barbie agreed to take over the lease on our apartment (her boyfriend Dave was going to move in), as well as keep Kitty-Bear.

The 21 hour train ride was mostly surreal. I met several other people of around the same age, I was 18 and they were in their late teens or early 20's. We spent most of that 21 hour train journey playing cards and watching the incredible scenery. We were on a train which had one long carriage with a glass dome instead of a roof and we spent many hours sitting under it and watching the Rocky Mountain's diverse splendour. The outside world raced past changing its display from bare rock, to densely wooded slopes, lakes shimmering in hues of green, blue and grey to snow capped peaks all in the time it took to play a few luxuriously slow hands of cards. The contrast of the speed of life flashing by outside the windows, to the decadence of the card game which was proceeding at a house cat's pace inside the train, was intriguing enough to make my brain flit in and out of both continuums with delight. I never played a hand myself, preferring to alternate between letting my mind wander off to swoop and whirl, speeding with the scenery flashing by outside and then flick back into the slower time inside the train to continue my observation of the card game in progress. At some point during those 21 hours on the train I slept, wrapped in the arms of a guy who wanted to make me his own. Desperate to be able to stretch out and sleep, we moved luggage from the bottom rack to the middle and top ones. Our high visibility and exhaustion prevented him from doing more than holding me close to him and once the train arrived in Banff, I parted from him after promising to call, knowing I had no intention of doing any such thing!

I spent what little money I had left on a taxi to the large hotel that had offered me a job as a chambermaid and accommodation. As soon as I arrived and introduced myself to the manager, I knew I had made a mistake. She looked at me, eyes tracing their disapproval from my wild hair to the hems of my rumpled jeans which ended in a soft fabric puddle around my shoes. She handed me a site map, hotel rules, uniform and out of hours dress rules and a work schedule finishing by informing me that if I left before my 3 month contract had finished, I would be blacklisted from ever working in any of the hotels in their chain. What a way to be greeted! I was due to start work the very next day so I wasted no time in walking the mile back into central Banff to look for another job.

I found a place to stay at the Youth Hostel and the next day found a job as a chambermaid at a motel nearby. I should have been delirious with relief at having successfully negotiated this first challenge in a new place but instead felt overwhelmed with all the changes. I found a pay phone and called mom to let her know I had arrived safely and ended up in tears when I told her how lonely I felt. I wasn't lonely exactly but didn't know what words to use to describe my angst.

'Well Denyse you spent a lot of time planning this move and you were certain this was what you wanted to do. There must be something else bothering you!'

'No.' I knew this answer wouldn't satisfy her so I said 'Yes, actually I don't have enough money to last till the end of the month.'

She sighed. 'What happened to your money?'

'I hated my boss at the hotel so I left and I have to rent a room at the hostel.'

'You've only been there one day, how can you hate her already?'

'She was like a total bitch mom! Anyway, I found another job so it's not like I was being lazy or anything!'

Silence.

'Mom?'

'I can lend you £50 till the end of the month.'

'Thanks mom, I really appreciate it!' I said pretending to be thrilled but wondering how I was going to manage to make that last until payday.

'Make sure I get that money back, I have none to spare and won't be able to give you anymore the next time you leave a job without another one to go to. That was plain silly of you to leave a job that paid for your food and accommodation without having another one to go to. I hope you've learnt a lesson!'

'I have mom, I promise I will pay you back!' The familiarity of her response to my seemingly irresponsible attitude with money had calmed me. I could never explain to her how frightening that woman had been, how my brain shut down from the sensory overload of her verbal bitterness and that I automatically I engaged my mouth before my brain. I no longer felt sad, just eager to escape her apparent disappointment in me once again and stride off on my own into the unknown. I have no idea how she found that money to put in my bank account but I made sure to pay her back from my first paycheque.

The motel where I worked as a chambermaid was spread out across quite a large area and so we used to move ourselves and equipment from the buildings on a motorised golf cart. I never managed to get the hang of driving these and would brake with my foot still on the accelerator, with the consequences you might expect! I dented many of these little vehicles on various obstacles around the compound, luckily none of these ever included customers cars or personal property or I would have been fired before I got a chance to inspect them damage. The manager must have had a blind spot where my lack of spatial awareness was concerned for he leant me his van one day to go into town. Driving back and rushed for time if I was to arrive before the start of my shift, I tried to squeeze the van down a side lane and scraped a long dent in the side of the van and a corresponding mark on the other car! I began dating the car driver shortly after this. He was one of my nicer dating disasters, a born again Christian and as determined not to have sex outside of marriage as I was to encourage him to do exactly that! He won the battle of wills much to my disgust and the relationship dwindled to an end. I began looking for another job the very day that I had to clean a room whose floors had been left covered in deep piles of vomit!

The first place I stopped in on my job hunt was a Japanese owned store called Saitoh Furs. I had seen their staff wanted sign in the window and was lucky enough to be hired straight away. An added bonus I thought was to be allowed live in their staff accommodation with the rent to be taken from my pay, one less thing for me to worry about and much closer than the youth hostel way up on top of the hill. I worked happily at the fur store for a few months, modelling the coats for rich Japanese businessmen who wanted to bring home a selection for their wives and mistresses. I began to pick up a few phrases in Japanese much to the appreciation of the customers who would coo over me as if I were a precocious child and photograph me in the furs they bought. At risk of angering the animal activists, I have to say the sensation of those furs on my skin was delicious and mostly indescribable. The Chinchilla furs felt like warm running water, Beaver fur caressed like the softest combination of sunlight clouds. The decadence of these feelings was marred by the fact that animals had been made to give up their lives to provide humans with the decadence they desired enough to pay extravagant sums for.

While working at this store my twin brother's Matthew and Gordon were born. I was vaguely puzzled at the concept of becoming a sister at the age of 19.

'Dad, do you realise that I will be almost 40 when they graduate?'

'And I will be on the wrong side of 60!' came his prompt reply.

Although puzzled, I was nonetheless thrilled at their arrival and promptly spent silly money on tiny leather moccasins for them. I had no idea what was an appropriate gift for a baby and thought they would look cute in them. It wasn't until years later when I had my own son and bought a similar pair of footwear that I realised that as cute as these shoes looked, they did not fit on baby feet easily and only then for a matter of weeks until the little feet grew too large to put into the soft leather.

I shared a room in Saitoh Fur's staff accommodation until they kicked me out for breaking the rules by adopting a sweet kitten. I found a room in a shared house and then, furious at being told to leave my previous accommodation, promptly began looking for another job, intending to punish them for their disregard of my needs by retaliating through leaving them one staff member short. I soon found work in a huge tobacconist and met a girl of my age named Connie with whom I would be inseparable for the next year. The house I lived in changed owners and they promptly instigated a no pet rule. Connie and I found a room to share in an apartment at the far end of town and worked 12 hour shifts, partying at the dance clubs until the early hours of the morning, often not arriving home until 4 am. I absolutely loved being on the dance floor, with the music vibrating up through my body and the lights playing across my vision. If raves had been invented at this point, I would undoubtedly have become a die hard fan! It is no wonder I burnt out after a year and I suspect it would have been much sooner if I had been drinking alcohol.

Connie and I partied with a dynamic group of people who all exuded differences, in fact some of them went out of their way to intentionally be as unique as possible, leaving my behaviours appearing quite normal in comparison. One of my favourite characters in our group was a flamboyant man named Sam. He was homosexual in a deliberately stereotypical fashion; camper than a row of tents, prone to hysterics and bitchier than anyone would think humanly possible. His extremes amused me no end and I would blatantly observe him for hours on end, secure in the knowledge that he liked me and therefore I was allowed to stare. Our group attracted attention and I began to sample men as if I had a revolving door in front of me. None lasted more than a night or two, no more than a few had anything beyond the ordinary to offer me. In amongst these men however, lurked my first experience of an orgasm (a sensation I thought I would never get to savour), a man with a penis so small and red in colour that it immediately brought the image of a crab-apple to mind (and who was exquisitely confident in all things sexual) and the revulsion I felt when I saw an uncircumcised adult penis for the first time.

I am sad to say that out of my whole Banff experience, a town which had a winter population of 600 and which swelled to accommodate 6000 in the tourist season, a town with views that ranged from sweeping flowered meadows dotted with grazing Buffalo, to snow capped mountains; my overwhelming memory is the shock of the pitiable comparison of the rumpled silk skinned flaccidness of an uncircumcised penis to the smooth tumescence of the average circumcised Canadian penis. I think it is obvious that I did not find the owner of this uncircumcised penis attractive and suspect that if I had then I would have found the appearance of the foreskin much more alluring! He was British by birth and had lived in Banff for many years. His nickname was 'Dawg' because he closely resembled the British bulldog in stature and shape of face. Dawg ran a pub in the centre of town and lived in a very nice house which included a hot tub as one of the perks of the job. He invited all of us round one morning after the pub had shut. We all crammed in the hot tub which was large enough to comfortably seat 8 but as we found, at a squish could hold ten and we ended up falling asleep in various locations of his place. The next morning I was awakened by the sound of him grunting as he stumbled through the living room where I had fallen asleep on the couch. He was on his way to the toilet, flaccid penis and long wrinkled foreskin on show for all who cared to look. I didn't and turned away to face the back of the couch but the rest of my dreams were tainted by limp, wrinkled, worm like creatures which flopped in monochrome tones across the usually vibrantly coloured canvas of my sleep.

It was during my time in Banff that the shocking news that HIV was a disease that was not restricted to homosexuals but could also be passed on through unprotected heterosexual intercourse. Up till then I had been living under the belief that the worst thing I could get from unprotected sex was herpes! Irrationally, instead of resolving to use condoms, I decided that the next guy that I began a sexual relationship with would be the man I would stay with forever. Problem solved? Hardly! Soon after this Connie and I met two tourists from Calgary, Paul and Steve, who were to cause us both angst in their own ways. Unbeknownst to us, Steve, the guy that Connie hooked up with was in a steady relationship. He must have thought there was no chance of being found out as Calgary was a few hours away from Banff. Paul was not the type of man I was usually attracted to, he was my height, stocky and very hairy. However, at the time, he seemed nice and Connie was involved with his best friend, so I ignored any warnings my logical mind may have been trying to project and embarked on a relationship that was doomed to fail from the start but would actually take 7 years to do so. I seem to routinely opt to travel along the path that offers the greatest resistance.

Like mother, like son

It wasn't until I gave birth to my son at 35 years old that I realised what true love felt like. My son was so much like me that I finally completely grasped the concept of empathy. I at long last, innately understood the concept that my life could be enhanced and enriched by ensuring the well being of another person. Talk about enlightenment.

By the time he was 16 months old, I was no longer the only person to notice that he was different from other children. The nursery was beginning to comment on some of TJ's unusual repetitive behaviours. They said that he would stand at the flip top bin for ages, opening and closing it instead of joining group sessions. When he was anxious for any reason he would organise the numerous tall paint pots, putting them into an order and then redoing it, completely focussed on his task and reluctant to come away. As he got older and stronger he increased his repetitive repertoire. He particularly loved a large foam couch which he would flip over and over all around the room, mowing down anyone in his way. At the time I worried that he was dreadfully unhappy but I now know he was simply 'stimming', a way of shutting down when the outside world got a bit too overwhelming, a way of going off into himself to process the overload of sensations. Eventually I would come to recognise that he was behaving exactly as I did as a child, during those episodes he was simply in an 'Arsenault' trance. This was the name we gave to this sort of behaviour on relatives from my mom's side of the family. We all had a tendency to go off into our own world or into an 'Arsenault' trance to varying degrees.

I tried without success to reassure the nursery staff that these behaviours were fairly common in my family and therefore should not be considered alarming. They were not convinced as he also would not do art work, refused to put his hands in anything squishy or messy and so on. I could quite understand his reluctance to do these things, hating the sensation myself and could not be less interested in doing arty stuff either. I tried to suggest to them that perhaps these just were not 'his thing'. They soon put me in my place by informing me that all children enjoy creating art to some extent. Oh really? That was news to me... There were also concerns about his lack of social skills for he appeared to crave the company of adults instead of joining in with the games other children were involved in.

At home he would line his cars and trucks up instead of driving them round and actively 'playing' with them. He couldn't pass a switch without flicking it up and down or side to side. He could spin for ages without falling over though I was certain that one time he would fall over and smack his head hard, vomit or both. TJ was not keen on change and without knowing it, he and I had become wrapped up in his rituals. He liked everything done in the same way and so mornings, evening and bedtimes flowed in a soothing predictable manner. I learned not to add inflections as I read his bedtime stories for I would have to make the exact same noises every time the story was read after that, and I would be admonished if I missed even a single word out. He had to roll his covers down to the end of the bed in an exact number of folds, usually 8 if he could manage it, before settling down with them pulled up over him, even in the summer, to get the first lot of his nightly naps. Much to my despair, he still woke a minimum of four times a night. He could not cope with bright sunshine which was easily resolved with the purchase of several pairs of sunglasses so there was always a pair to hand.

TJ also developed an obsession with keeping the car doors locked and the windows closed if the car was moving. I had a car with no air-conditioning and so we sweltered in the summer to the point where I began to feel this was becoming a dangerous situation. I spent hours discussing these behaviours with Chris and he would come up with ingenious suggestions such as buying TJ a portable radio with ear plugs for in car use to block the noise from the open windows. The suggestions worked and solved the problem of travelling in a car with no fresh air but did not change the root cause of these and the many other unusual behaviours that TJ would parade around as if he were a mobile stage show. Like all children though he showed a remarkable ability to bringing out his most unique ones and undesirable behaviours at the most unwelcome times with impeccable timing. Eventually he was referred to a community paediatrician who said she was certain he was behaving as if he has Asperger's syndrome.

I have been told that for most parents this is a huge shock and terribly upsetting but I grasped onto those words with a desperate greed. Here was a name for his behaviours, something I could look up and learn about. Something that surely would have techniques and treatment which could be applied to help TJ cope better. I joined our local autism support network and realised that there were many children and several adults in the same city who behaved in similar ways to TJ and where we were immediately accepted and invited to join them on outings to local events. A door had to been opened to whole new world and it was a good place to be.

A parallel world

The more time we spent with the local autism network, the more I realised that I was a part of it in more ways than simply as a mother of a child on the autistic spectrum. I had begun to strongly suspect that I was on the spectrum too but did not feel able to tell anyone yet. I was too focussed on seeking help for TJ's benefit and I was more than happy to shove my needs behind me so that his could be met. I had always been like this with TJ, from the moment of his birth and wondered how I could have not wanted to have a child for so many years. Being a mother was the most amazingly rewarding experience of my life though the desire to make his life perfect and the frustration of not being able to achieve this was a painful lesson that I kept learning. I could not understand why his birth father did not show more interest in him. Although I never refused him access, he was not allowed unsupervised contact with TJ (another story and one which I do not need to tell as it is a matter of public record for those who know where to look for such things). I was given special training in order to be competent to supervise their contact and endured it whenever he wanted to see TJ as I thought that TJ should be able to have contact with his birth father. The shine soon wore off as TJ became more challenging and less compliant and his visits were becoming increasingly sporadic. In September of 2007 I realised that he had only visited TJ five times that year. For a child who disliked change these visit were more disruptive than of any benefit and I gave him an ultimatum to either see TJ weekly or to stop altogether. He chose the latter.

Although I feel that this is in TJ's best interest I can not understand how this man who provided half of TJ's genetic makeup could think that was a preferable option. I feel as if I would die if TJ was not 100% part of my life. Each illness he has, hurts me somewhere deep inside where the scars don't show, every time he bumps himself I feel like crying too, when he is sad I want to catch the moon if only to see him smile again. When he is rejected, my heart rips open a little too. Yet even with all this shared pain I would have my life no other way and I have learned that just because someone's sperm helped to make a child does not automatically mean that man is a father. Even if I had stayed with him he would never have become TJ's father in the true sense of the word. He lacked the innate selflessness that is required to become a good parent, he deeply desired an easy life and this was not going to be something that TJ could accommodate. With the clarity of hindsight I now wish that I had run far away from him as soon as I discovered that I was pregnant. However I didn't and now he is named as TJ's father on his birth certificate even though he is the furthest thing possible from a real father.

The man who raises you with clearly defined and calmly reinforced behavioural boundaries, who shares in your pain, holds you when you are ill, plays with you in sun, wind and rain, teaches you the joy of laughter, shares your good and bad times is a real father. Chris and I had been in a relationship since TJ was 2 years old and by this point had become TJ's father. The positive changes in TJ were obvious to all. In fact we had both been lacking a reliable positive male influence and parenting became much easier with Chris's constant support. Together we rejoiced in being granted the privilege of seeing the world through TJ's eyes, children make the most marvellous leaps of intuition and I suppose we must have all done the same but simply do not remember. Having my child show me what I had forgotten so long ago, is the greatest blessing I have ever been granted.

Chris never passed critical comment on my behaviours as all previous boyfriends had done. He was content to accept me as I was and seemed to understand that I could find a light touch so ticklish that it was almost painful. That sometimes I would hold onto him as if I would have to be prised away and other times I could only manage a fleeting hug. He accepted that this was not a personal rejection of his affections but simply a case of me being overwhelmed by my heightened senses. He learned to touch me in a way I could cope with, in a way that was simply exquisite in every sense. He did not feel threatened or unloved when I drifted off into deep thoughtful silences at the end of the day or wanted to read beside him instead of watching TV with him. I longed to be near him when we were apart and TJ despaired when he was not there with us.

Chris has two boys of his own and often had them stay over at his house which meant we had to spend those nights apart. TJ has never been good at coping with change but he began to miss Chris to such an extent that we began to seriously consider buying a house large enough for all of us to live in together. Finding a place that pleased all of us was more complicated that we expected but eventually we found a large house that we could afford in a good neighbourhood with an excellent school for TJ to attend once he finished pre-school. Moving in with Chris was a life enhancing experience for TJ and I. Each day I wake thankful that he is a part of our lives and each night I am eager to get under the covers with him. Thanks to Chris, TJ is learning skills I would not be able to teach him, like how to understand when others are joking. He was still demanding and firmly adherent to his rituals but we were all learning to cope with them a little better now that we had gelled together as a full time team. The real challenges arose when one of us was one our own with TJ.

An evening Chez Aspie
(Aspie is a nickname that people with Asperger's syndrome sometimes use to refer to themselves)

TJ still wakes frequently throughout the night, he has always been a restless sleeper but on this particular day he had woken 600 trillion and ten times the night before.

He proclaimed and blamed a variety of things; 'my bed hurt me, my room is wibbling, when you shut the door the voices start, when you close my door it gets noisy in here, there are shadows in here, I am awake so you should be too, there is a fly in here, it is too loud, get it outtttttttttt!!!!!!!!' etc and so on ad infinitem.

What was unusual was the fact that he was such a good boy in the morning (except perhaps for the bit where he insisted on Special K red berries, with no red bits which ended with me eating that bowl full and him grumpily eating porridge)! Well, he was as good as any four year old could be expected to be and that is exceptionally well behaved for TJ! Now let me tell you the lesson I learned that day...

He wasn't being good! He was biding his time, lulling me into a false sense of security by conserving his energy in order to be really challenging that evening! When he knew I would be on my own, meaning no Chris at supper or bedtime, meaning a change in his routine, which is not acceptable in the parallel world he lives in. I should have known better, far too gullible at my age really...

He kicked off when I picked him up from school instead of Chris, who has been doing this since I tried to surgically remove my own toe nail with the aid of a concrete block. I can drive short distances but have been avoiding doing it more than once a day because at the end of the car drive is a long path to his school.

So my first conversation with 'changeling' boy since leaving him at school this morning went something like this:

Me: (big smile, outstretched arms) 'Hello darling, did you have a nice day today?'

TJ: (Grinding to a halt, looking pissed off) 'Where is Daddy?!'

Me: (Mentally cringe, remember we hadn't begun preparation for change to routine) 'Daddy's getting ready for going out with Uncle Malcom tonight

TJ: (Hands on hips in decidedly camp fashion, stamps feet with same affect)

'Nooo, I want daddy, I don't WANT him to go out tonight; I want to give him a hug and a kiss!'

Me: 'Well if we hurry home we might get there in time for you to give him a hug and kiss before he goes' (note his forehead furrowing into line of non-compliance and say hurriedly) 'Is there a boy here who would like to unlock the car for me?'

(Pat myself on back as he grabs keys and willingly walks up long path to road where our car is parked)

Second conversation:

Me: (After strapping his seat belt on and limping on my broken toe round to my side) 'Lets open the windows, it is so hot in here!' (cursing silently as I remember that I forgot to change the dead batteries in his hand held radio)

TJ: (Putting sunglasses on and pulling blue fleece blanket over head and body after realising the radio still not working) 'I don't WANT the windows open, I WANT daddy to stay home.'

Me: 'Okaaaaayyy, suit yourself, blanket boy!' (Open window on my side and roof hatch, drive home, hoping to get there before Chris goes and waiting for TJ to pass out from heat exhaustion so I can remove blue fleece blanket)

We get home in time to see Chris standing outside waiting for taxi, berate lack of parking spaces with a myriad of harsh sounding but not actual curse words (just in case they get repeated by blanket boy to his teacher), 'Pants, flipper, sherbet!' , find parking space on other side of road. TJ sheds the blanket and much to his disgust I hold his hand as we cross the road, then let go so he can run up the path to Chris who lifts him up, way up for a big hug, tears of relief in my eyes, sweat on Chris's forehead... well it's his own fault! He is wearing a suit, long sleeved shirt and a tie!!!

The taxi pulls up with the other suits in it and off they go, no doubt muttering importantly to themselves of new candidates, secret handshakes, initiation rituals, speeches, oranges, goose fat (okay I made the last two up)... all of which I have learned to interpret as meaning: a great excuse for a regular meal and drinks with mates! (Not that I am forgetting their dedication to numerous charitable good works, just trying to keep things in perspective!)

I spend the evening vacuuming accompanied by the dulcet tones of TJ shrieking that the noise is too loud and simultaneously demanding that he be allowed to do the hovering.

I make supper accompanied by a running commentary of 'Why can't I use the big knife to help cut up the peppers? I am a big boy, I can use a knife!'

I fend off a blanket covered whirling dervish, wondering for the millionth time why he doesn't he fall down dizzy after a while like everyone else. I cajole TJ into removing blanket with promises of being allowed to scoop ice cream (a huge thrill for some inexplicable reason), if he is sensible at supper. The blanket vanishes and he proceeds to insist he does not want to eat pizza with red peppers on it, which are, apparently, perfectly acceptable if picked off, lined up in a precise fashion on his plate and then dipped in mustard before being eaten! Watching him reminds me, yet again, that I used to be just like him as a child and at that point, I send a smile across the table to him, only to be confronted with 'I am fed up with smiles today!'

Shortly after this evening I explained to Chris my certainty that I too had Asperger's syndrome and that I wanted to be assessed and, if possible, diagnosed. He accepted this revelation with his usual calmness. I had recently changed job, although by this stage in my life I had learnt not to leave one before I had another to go to! I had gone from working as a midwife in a very busy maternity unit to teaching student midwives at a local university. This move had given me the emotional space to take a step back and examine my behaviours from different angles. Previously I had been unable to do this adequately while working in the NHS due to the mist which the constant stress left in layers in my brain. I was so addled and exhausted by the end of my shift that I was unable to reflect on, to thoroughly examine and deliberate over my behaviours and the reasons for why I felt and behaved the ways I did.

My high functioning label

In short order, my GP had referred me to the national Autism Society's assessment and diagnostic centre. I give him a lot of credit for going ahead with this. I had been the surgery midwife a few years before this and it was difficult for him to accept that I could be on the autistic spectrum when I had once appeared to be a fully functioning member of their team. I am happy to say that I certain he has altered his opinion about what people with Asperger's syndrome are capable of since then. I was invited for an assessment and they strongly recommended that I bring Chris with me. He was very uncomfortable with this concept as he felt he might have to talk about me whereas I thought this was a great idea as it would give another perspective on my behaviours. At the end of the assessment I was told by Dr Gould that she was certain I had Asperger's syndrome and spent some time checking how I and Chris felt about my diagnosis. I was thrilled to have my suspicion's confirmed and to know that there were people out there just like me, I too had a social niche. I was in a bit of a quandary about 'coming out Asperger's' at work but when I eventually did do so, I received a very favourable response and then everyone carried on as if nothing had changed. Which of course it hadn't I am still the same person I was before I disclosed my 'disability'. Of course I do have a 'High Functioning' autistic label now and I feel that this has both benefits and disadvantages to it no even though overall I have found that being diagnosed with Asperger's syndrome has life enhancing.

Confused? Let me try to explain...

Let me introduce you to my 'High Functioning' label, as I said above it came attached to my diagnosis of Asperger's syndrome. It seems to serve many purposes for people who like to discuss me. What it does for me is less clear, depending often on others' Points of View. I am told the ones who get labelled as children have more chance of their Autism diagnosis being taken seriously. It also seems that my 'High Functioning' label has the power to make my Autism 'mild' and less real.

In discussions about 'High Functioning' people like myself, I sometimes get told that that I am Notlikeyourchild (NLYC). NLYC is simply another name for 'High Functioning Autism'. Though I too may have 'stimmed' (a repetitive habit that releases endorphins and calms Autistic people) by spinning in circles, hitting and pinching myself, rocking myself, digging my nails in the palm of my own hand, sucking my thumb and stepping from foot to foot as a child, I no longer do any of these things (at least not that anyone knows about). Chewing the insides of my cheek, chewing gum, tapping my pen, folding the edges of book pages under my thumb nail as I read, smoking, these are all adult forms of 'stimming'. Therefore, because I have learnt to outwardly behave as a neurotypical person, many people assume I can not possibly have Autism, at least not to the severity that their child does. Oh really? Since when did it become a competition? Do they not think that with that kind of attitude they may be doing their child a disservice, perhaps preventing their child from reaching their full potential?

I, like other persons with this form of Autism, do not self injure in a commonly recognised form. I may have a history of inappropriate behaviours which stem from my inability to sort risky from safe, such as preferring 'unprotected' sex because I find condoms uncomfortable, smoking with great pleasure from the time I was 12 and drinking lots during my first marriage as a coping mechanism. These get labelled as self abusive behaviour as if I have made a sensibly informed decision to inflict damage upon myself. I may have damage to vital organs from drinking too much alcohol during that time, eating too much of the wrong kinds of food and smoking too many cigarettes. I say these activities were another form of 'stimming' but because neurotypical people do them too, these do not count. I am 'High Functioning'; therefore these things must have nothing to do with my Autism.

Apparently I should really know better... The fact that I managed to quit smoking and now drink a sensible amount only serve to prove that I did not need any help. I get told, better late than never! I disagree! I sense people weighing up my behaviours, comparing to their own and I can not have a disability because they too have done some of the same things and to the same degree. The key word here folks, is, some. If I had the guidance I needed many years ago, I would have had understood sooner that 'stimming' in a socially accepted fashion, like drinking and smoking, as compared to thumb sucking are not necessarily better for me.

I have self care skills which are adequate, sometime better than that, after all I have finally learnt that there are consequences if I don't pay my bills on time and so I don't spend more than I earn. That is down to fear, rather than neurotypical adult responsibility. The bills I forgot to pay in my early adult years and current inability to stop overeating are apparent evidence of what many call my irresponsibility. I say I am not being irresponsible, I know I am 'stimming' when I eat inappropriate amounts and it is an incredibly hard thing to stop doing, harder than not smoking it seems. My High Functioning label does not support me in modifying my behaviour. When I spoke to others of my reluctance as a child to throw anything away, because all my treasures were equally precious, this was seen as result of laziness, of deliberately wilful and disobedient behaviour, not Autism. Asperger's was not recognised as existing or as a part of the autistic spectrum until the early 1980's.

Too late to have been any help in rescuing me from myself.

I also get told, on occasion, by people who know someone who has an autistic child, that people with 'Real' Autism lack self care skills on a more fundamental level, because, of course, they know of what they speak! I communicate well because I constantly practice communication skills as a form of reinforcement. At 40, I suspect most people do not need to rehearse greeting people appropriately but I do it daily. This practice ensures that I can keep my job and pass as mostly 'normal' in the workplace, where I can avoid anything other than the most basic of social interaction. I struggle with social verbal discourse but I am an effective public speaker. My 'High Functioning' Label makes it a challenge to use this skill to speak about Autism though. When I try I am sometimes subjected to criticism and ridicule for daring to compare myself to other people's apparently more obviously 'disabled' children. Asperger's is quite rightly called the 'Hidden' disability.

Sometimes, my 'High Functioning' abilities prevent me from obviously needing extra accommodations in the workplace. Often, I will struggle to maintain a facade of neurotypical behaviours at work. Unless a person has distinctive features, I struggle to recognise faces for far longer than is considered acceptable. To compensate for this I will jot notes in the back of a book to help me 'recognise' co-workers though I have run into problems before when my jottings have been discovered. This is because I write things like; *Tony – hair too black to be natural*, or *Amy- flicks blonde hair a lot, wears tight shirts with a bra that appears to be too small* and *Maggie- always has panty lines and laughs too loud* and so on. These are for my benefit to help me do my job better by being able to acknowledge co –workers but although these examples are fictitious, I can see why real life types of these notes would upset people. I have to learn to not leave the book lying around where it can be read by anyone but me.

I may misunderstand instructions, directions or may have difficulty relating to co-workers. I may misinterpret the culture of the business I work for, making remarks which are 'inappropriate' and I try to avoid attending work social functions. I am often outspoken at meetings and demand to adhere to the set agenda because I think to do otherwise is a dreadful waste of my work time. I am there to attend to the meeting agenda, not to waste time on social niceties. As I mentioned previously, a meeting is not a social occasion; it is an expenditure of people's time and a commodity which I do not have to spare during my working day. I expect the agenda and timings to be adhered to as these are what I have allocated for in my diary. Contrary to what some seem to believe of me in the work place, it isn't that I don't care about my colleagues, I just happen to be very focussed on the task at hand

When I get reprimanded, my 'High Functioning' label is there to remind me (and everyone else who is aware of my label) that this is my own fault. When I protest that failure to accommodate my Autism may be at least a part of the problem, everyone looks at me in disbelief. I did not disclose my disability to my new employers during my interview. I was scared of what the reaction would be if I 'came out Asperger's' to them, though I have since 'disclosed' to them and now know that I shouldn't have been worried. They were aware of my reputation as someone who can get the job done in my chosen field.

In fact I am considered a success in my chosen career pathway and I have achieved this without support from the agencies whose job it is to guide me through behaviour modifications, independent living and work skills. However when I worked for the NHS previously my nerves were in tatters at the beginning and end of most workdays from the effort of maintaining my neurotypical disguise. I am fixated on my memory of what it was like to work for my last manager and how she would have treated me if my disability had been known back then. I still have nightmares of being shunned if I disclose my 'disability' to my new colleagues and of course to new employers as I will change jobs many, many times before retirement. I seem to have no staying power at jobs and always give in to the urge to find a new job before I am exposed as the fraud I know I am. Overcoming deeply inbuilt feelings of inadequacy are one of my biggest challenges!

My 'High Functioning' label... I have yet to discover whether it is a blessing or a curse. I strongly suspect a little bit of both. However I am happy to have been diagnosed. My diagnosis means that I can demonstrate to others a good example of what is achievable with or without a diagnosed 'disability'. Although I am worried about disclosing my diagnosis to new employers and colleagues, I have no qualms about anyone else knowing and hope that this book has helped others to understand the 'hidden' facets of Aspergers.

The end? Of course not.

I thought I should write a bit more about what it is to be an adult with a disability instead of just my childhood memories. That got me thinking about the reactions I've had when I disclose that I have/am a form of Autism called Asperger's syndrome. The reactions I have had from people I have disclosed to since my diagnosis last year have ranged mostly from quiet disbelief to defiant outrage. I assume that by expressing disbelief when I tell them that I have a disability they are trying to be kind. However it is not kind, it makes a mockery of what I endure on a daily basis in order to function as a member of society.

I have been told that I couldn't possibly have Asperger's because 'those people can't work at high functioning jobs like yours'. What they don't see is the amount of rehearsing I do each morning, in order to practice appropriate social etiquette to help me avoid making an irreparable faux pas at work, so that I can keep this job that pays my bills. They don't see me crying in the toilets at work from sheer sensory overload.

Sensory overload is horrible; it feels like my brain is being jabbed with cocktail sticks, or like my skin is being scratched by a pin or rubbed with sandpaper. It makes me irritable at best and a sobbing depressed wreck at worst. I suffer with lack of facial recognition; can you imagine having to struggle to match face to job every single working day? The thought of going to work each day makes me want to scream with frustration.

I have been told that I can't have Asperger's syndrome because of the fact that I am in love with a wonderful man. They don't see or have chosen to disregard the string of failed relationships before this one relationship that works so well. They don't know the internal dynamics of our relationship, of Chris's endless patience with my behaviours, of his acceptance that I am a grown woman who needs a lover that can also be my carer on social occasions, that I am as vulnerable socially as a young girl. They don't know that I love him so much that I am willing to take care not to step on his feelings too often, to make the effort to show him just how much I do care. No... people just see the external perfect gloss of our love, not the hard work that brought the shine through the rust. They make the assumption that it is an effortless relationship (does such a thing really exist?) and not one that someone with my disability could ever achieve.

Asperger's syndrome is sometimes referred to as 'the hidden disability' for the reasons I listed above. I have learnt to pass as a mostly mainstream individual and I sometimes wonder if I have done myself a disservice. It would be nice to be praised for the achievements I have made despite or perhaps because of my disability. For it to be acknowledged that is extra hard for me to achieve the same goals as the majority of my co-workers.

I think that I went on to achieve as much as I have because I had no other option. I felt trapped at home, desperate for as long as I can remember to be an adult. To get away from the noise, disorganisation, emotional pain and chaos of my childhood. I wanted to leave home from an early age and to be able to do that I had to be able to support myself. So I did just that, albeit making many mistakes along the way and perhaps surviving to this age through sheer luck on many occasions but here I am to tell the tale.

I believe that 'disabled' should be called 'differently abled', regardless of what the diagnosis may be. If someone wants something strongly enough, then they can achieve a personally acceptable semblance of their goal with the right support and determination. I have been writing since a young age to try and express how differently I saw the world. My writing has improved a lot over the years, people even say they enjoy reading what I write. Writing helps me make sense of my world and the world of neurotypical people and now it also helps me to escape. As well as this book, I am using the publication of my first fiction novel 'Without Alice' in 2009 as another way to help me raise autism awareness.

Knowing where to end this memoir is quite challenging as, of course, at this time there is no end. I am very much alive and am, for the first time, learning how to enjoy my life. I am in a wonderful relationship and have a son and 2 step sons, something many people assume someone with Asperger's is incapable of. How I got to this stage of my life would need another whole book to tell the story adequately. I began this in an attempt to show how very different my world is and how is it possible to cope and achieve despite or perhaps because of my 'disability'. In some ways I feel is has been an advantage for me to have an autistic spectrum disorder, it has allowed me to move on, relatively unscathed from situations that would have psychologically injured others and in other ways it has been a disadvantage for the same reason, certainly in relation to forming good relationships with others.

For all of you reading this, who are on the autistic spectrum or have children on the spectrum or simply know of someone who is on the spectrum, believe me when I tell you this; you or they are special. I think of us as the 'Chameleon people', we have an amazing ability to morph into the guise of neurotypical behaviour for periods of time if and when we chose to do so. This allows us to function in mainstream society although admittedly it is a challenge at all times.

I believe that we can achieve anything we wish as long as we make sure the right modifications are in place to help us along the way. This may mean years of hard work but I promise you, in the end, all your efforts will be rewarded by increased confidence and you will surprise yourself with what you learn along the way. Everyone struggles sometimes but what matters is the attitude you have about it. If you want to get on and do things and are willing to work at it, then you will succeed. You must be the measure of your own successes for only you will know how hard you worked to achieve them. Enjoy your life, it doesn't matter if you struggle as long as you stay proud of what you achieve and that keep trying to surprise yourself with new successes.

Acknowledgements

I would like to thank TJ for being my son. TJ, I have marvelled at your wonderfulness every day since you were born. There are bits of my love for you in every book I write. I love you all up…forever… no matter what.

I would like to thank Chris for his unconditional love and encouragement. I love you with every beat of my heart.

I would like to thank all the strong women in my family who loved me and encouraged me to write out my feelings. I love you right back.

I would like to thank my dad for his quiet strength and beautifully descriptive letters, within which I found my writing 'voice'. For this gift, I am grateful and love you beyond words.

I would like to thank my step mother for telling me that I should get on with writing a book and submitting it to a publisher and for reminding me that the worst that could happen would be that they would say 'no thank you'. I love you for giving me 'bravery by proxy'.

I would like to say thank you to all my blog readers who have commented on excerpts of this book for the past year.

Thanks also to bluechrome, the publisher of my fiction novel *Without Alice* (due out in 2009), for their help, advice and support with the layout of this book and the front and back covers.

Caroline Smailes, novelist and founder of BubbleCow.co.uk, the online editorial service, thank you so much for all your advice, encouragement and friendship. Last but not least, a big thank you to the Arts Council, Youwriteon.com and Legend Press who have made the printing of this collection of my memories a reality.

The obligatory 'author bio' page

I began writing at an early age and plan to keep at it as long as I find it enjoyable. I've had several short stories published in various anthologies and spent the past year and a half writing a monthly academic column on preconception care, pregnancy and beyond for FaM-ily magazine.

I do have a low boredom threshold and am therefore currently writing two fiction novels 'The Plump WAG's Club', 'The Garden of Eden', 'The Bohemian Crockpot' a collection of recipes from my childhood and finally, 'Maverick' which is an ever increasing compilation of my short stories and poems.

Obviously all of the above is not enough to keep me busy and so, in between enjoying time with my family, working full time and writing (during the hours when I probably should be sleeping), I spend time on my blogs and website.

My blogs, website and email address:

http://djkirkby.blogspot.com/
http://anaspiereviews.blogspot.com/
http://namlessnovel.blogspot.com/
http://benchpics.blogspot.com/
http://exquisitedreams.org/books.aspx
djkirkby@gmail.com

Please come by and say hello

Lightning Source UK Ltd.
Milton Keynes UK
07 September 2009

143434UK00002B/301/P